#1023 Fiction

DATE DUE

12-11-03	#14		

LOST RIVER BRIDGE

Lost River Bridge

as told by
Elijah Taber

Copyright © 2001 Stephen P. Byers

All rights reserved. No part of this book may be reproduced or transmitted in any form or by any means, electronic or mechanical, including photocopying, recording, or by any information storage and retrieval system without permission in writing from the copyright owner, except for the inclusion of brief quotations in a review or article.

This is a work of fiction. Names, characters, places and incidents are either the product of the author's imagination or are used fictitiously. Any resemblance to any actual person living or dead, events or locales is entirely coincidental.

ISBN: 1-929663-02-1

Library of Congress Catalog Card Number: 00-193482

Published by:

16 Lockerbie Lane
Bella Vista, Arkansas 72715-3501

Printed in the United States by:
RJ Communications
51 East 42nd Street, Suite 1202
New York, NY 10017

To my grandchildren

Andrew
Stephen
Mary Elspeth
Matthew
Mitchell
Brett

And to my mentor ... my father

    This book results from ten years of storytelling, an adventure I began after I retired from the business world. Soon after I started I realized I did not want to tell other people's stories; I wanted to tell my own. Not all the tales in this book are original. Some come from my father's repertoire that I felt duty bound to include for whatever storytelling skills I have, I owe to him. I was fascinated doing my research to find stories that he told me as a child reproduced in various places. That, I suppose, is to be expected for storytelling is the obligation to pass on our history and our foibles learned in childhood to the generation that follows us.

Other books by Stephen P. Byers

The Naked Jaybird
ISBN 1-929663-00-5
A mystery of international intrigue
that would destroy America

Bent Coin
ISBN 1- 929663-01-3
A story of greed and altruism, deceit and naiveté
between two people whose lives become inextricably entwined

Available from the publisher at
http://www.booksbybyers.com

Books by Byers
16 Lockerbie Lane
Bella Vista, Arkansas 72715-3501

LOST RIVER BRIDGE

**A novel by
Stephen P. Byers
In 20 Episodes**

PART 1 - 1946

1	The River Flows Uphill	13
2	Lost River Bridge	21
3	Aunt Lizzie	31
4	The Pursey Boys	39
5	Making Money	46
6	Elijah T. Pursey	53
7	Abby Watson	60
8	Abner's Dogs	67
9	Herman and Gerda	72
10	Farewell	81

PART 2 – 1988

11	Mother Love	89
12	The Beginning of the End	97
13	Deceit	106
14	The Truth about Doc	113
15	Annie	122
16	Something Did Happen	127
17	A True Story	134
18	The Mallow Birds	141
19	What about the Cemetery?	151
20	The Disciples	155

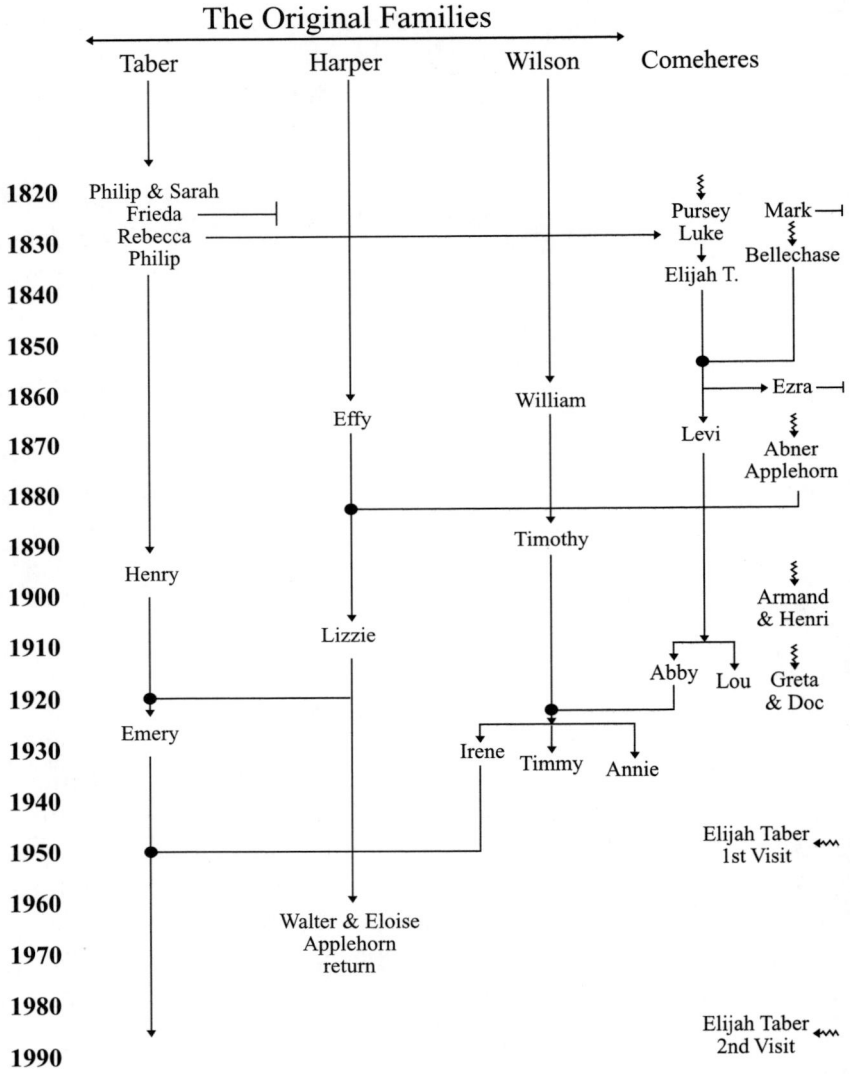

Elijah Taber

Elijah Taber stumbled into my imagination in Canada—British Columbia, to be exact. He arrived on a July day in 1994 while my wife and I summered at the Lake of the Woods, about three kilometers north of Hope, at the southern end of the Fraser River Canyon. At seventy years of age, the poor man had escaped from more than fifty years of routine toil. He had forgotten his beginnings, his middles and his endings. I found him depressed on the day of his incarnation, alone not knowing where his search might lead. In his loneliness, he asked me to provide a heritage, a family with experiences he could remember.

What would you have done? Denied him? Surely not! I confided in him, allowed him to peek at my ancestry, confessing long-buried secrets from my past. Frankly, I allowed him to steal my stories. Alas, he is a bounder. He not only took my tales he expanded them.

"Elijah," I scolded one day, "you have warped my stories to suit yourself. You have imbued them with details that may not be true."

"Rubbish," he responded. "I refuse to accept your objections. After all, I am only a reflection of you."

"What about Lost River Bridge?"

"It is the essence of solitude enfolding its own society viewed through the utopian spectacles of my mind. It reflects contentment and discomfort, peace and noise, goodwill and hardship. It is, in fact, the equal of the little town in the Eastern Townships."

I leave you to make your way along Elijah's trail. I deny all responsibility for his actions and will not vouch for the truth of his tales. You are on your own to judge him as you may. I have only this to say, he is a pleasant comrade. I know him well and I enjoy his stories.

Stephen P. Byers
Bella Vista
Summer 2000

Life's but a walking shadow, a poor player
That struts and frets his hour upon the stage
And then is heard no more: it is a tale
Told by an idiot, full of sound and fury
Signifying nothing.

                                      Shakespeare

PART ONE

1946

Episode One

The River Flows Uphill

The troop train from Halifax stopped at a siding near an abandoned athletic stadium in Montreal. Four hundred soldiers burst from the coaches. Relatives crowded the playing field that had been cleared of snow. I walked through the throng, and across the field where I broke my arm six years before playing high school football. My mother stood near the goal posts. We looked at each other, not knowing what to say. Then we embraced.

Home at last! The two of us sat at the kitchen table. She served coffee. My hand trembled as I tried to lift the cup. She looked away and wiped her eyes. When she turned back, I was drinking, holding the cup in two hands. By April, I achieved a degree of comfort at home, but the war had not faded from my memory.

"You've been home for a few months," she said one morning, "but you're still edgy. I think some travel might be good for you. Visit some army pals; call on our relatives. College doesn't start until September. You need to escape, to expel the images that crowd your mind. You can't go on forever talking, thinking, and dreaming war."

"Would you like to come with me?"

"No. That would defeat the purpose. It'll be better if you go alone. I'd make your trip uncomfortable."

"Where do you think I should go?"

"Ontario. Alberta. You might consider the Tabers in Missouri."

I took Mother's advice. I bounced from my relatives in Ontario to those in Alberta asking each what they knew of the Missouri Tabers. I remembered my father, who died in 1942, reading

STEPHEN P. BYERS

Kipling's "Just So Stories" aloud when I was a child. My favorite was the Elephant's Child who was ever so curious about what the crocodile had for lunch. He asked all of his relations each of whom spanked him exceedingly hard for his curiosity, and did not answer his question. When I let my sense of humor get the better of me, I asked my Canadian relations, "Do you know what the crocodile eats for dinner?" As you might suspect, I drew curious comments about my head wound so I changed my question to, "Have you ever met the Missouri Tabers?"

I usually received one of two answers. The more common; "Does your head hurt a lot?" The other, "Missouri Tabers? Who are they?"

I waved goodbye with a genial smile and set off on my journey like the Elephant's Child on the way to the *great, green, greasy Limpopo River* to discover what the crocodile ate for dinner.

The branches of the family tree divided almost two hundred years ago. Uprooted and choosing separate worlds, the branches found new roots and forgot the trunk that once united them. Filled with a spirit of adventure, I felt the urge to track my kin as if drawn by an astrological force. I knew they lived at Lost River Bridge in Missouri, an unidentifiable place on any map I examined. In late June, I flew to Kansas City with no preparation, invitation, or plan of action.

Inquiring at travel agencies and tourist bureaus along my route, my question changed to, "Ever heard of Lost River Bridge?"

The curious glances and vague responses ranged from, "Never heard of it," to, "I think maybe in the south somewhere." At least the condition of my head escaped curiosity.

If any organization could locate anyone in America, surely it was the Bell Telephone Company. The cultivated inflection of the operator asked, "Whom are you trying to contact?"

"Henry Taber," I answered, "in Lost River Bridge, Missouri."

"I'm sorry, sir. We have no such place listed in the directory."

Thus, I embarked on my search of Southern Missouri with no more definition of my destination than the Elephant's Child. The bus to Springfield made countless stops on its protracted eight-hour

LOST RIVER BRIDGE

trip. I studied my map as the countryside drifted by. In the hope that some higher power might guide my choice, I selected Gainesville, the seat of Ozark County, as a likely place to find the trail of the lost Taber tribe. The gods smiled on me; I succeeded with my first telephone call.

"I'm on my way to visit you, Uncle Henry," I said after he recovered from his surprise. "I need directions on how to find you."

"Carry on to Gainesville," he shouted as if not realizing a wire connected us. "We're 'bout fifteen miles northeast; maybe more, I ain't sure. When you're half way 'tween Gainesville an' ... an' ... just a minute." His bellow to Aunt Lizzie almost burst my eardrums. "This here is Elijah Taber from Canada ... I don't know. I'll ask him. Elijah! You still there?"

"Yes." I pictured Aunt Lizzie a mile or two off in the woods.

"Lizzie wants to know where you're at."

"I'm in a telephone booth in Springfield."

"He's in a telephone booth in Springfield ... What'd you say, Lizzie? ... Oh! She wants to know if you're coming here."

The bellowing annoyed me as I jammed quarters in the slot, but asking him to lower his voice would only prolong the agony.

"Uncle Henry, this is costing me a fortune. All I want is directions on how to get to your place."

"You got a car?"

"No."

"You cain't get here from there if you ain't got no car." For a moment, I thought I was in New England. I felt the urge to tell him he had the expression reversed, but declined to say what I knew he would never understand.

"Okay. I'll get a car. Now tell me how to find you."

I listened to him discuss the directions with Aunt Lizzie at the top of his voice. Nine more quarters appeased the operator.

"Elijah! She cain't 'member. Anyway, when you're half way 'tween that other place and Gainesville, look for a dog."

The question was too obvious. I didn't want to ask, but then, on second thought, I had no choice.

"What color dog?"

"Ain't rightly sure. He's a big fellow, all right."

"I'm sure he is, but tell me this, Uncle Henry. How will I know when I'm half way if I don't know the name of the other town even if I do see a big dog?"

When the Elephant's Child arrived at the banks of the *great, green, greasy Limpopo River* and asked his question, the crocodile clamped his jaws on the nose of Elephant's Child and answered that he'd have Elephant's Child today; and there was no escape. I had indeed fallen into the same trap unable to avoid being consumed with inane responses.

"'Cause our road is right there; on the right like I told you."

"Is it the only road? There's no other road that turns to the right?" I could feel the pain of the crocodile's teeth.

"Oh, sure there is," he said, "lots of them."

"How will I know which one it is, then?"

"I just told you. It's the one that's half way."

"Thanks Uncle Henry. Tell Aunt Lizzie I'll be there for supper in two days."

I bought a car. In exchange for one hundred thirty-five dollars and eighty-six cents, I owned a 1936 six-cylinder Studebaker. I found a boarding house where I could eat my meals and ask questions. Puzzled frowns accompanied vacant looks until Lost River Bridge became the only topic of conversation at the dining room table. A drummer said he'd been there once.

"That's the place where the river runs in two directions."

"What do you mean?"

"The main body of the river on the south side flows from west to east. On the north side, it flows from east to west."

"Naturally," I said. "Did you know most rivers in Canada flow uphill?"

"Is that right?"

Thoughts of war were never far from my mind in those days. They filtered in and out of focus as I searched for the turnoff to Lost River Bridge. I made my choice and hoped the gods who steered me to Gainesville would not abandon me now. I followed the twists and turns through old oak and hickory timber. Eventually, a delta, thick with weeds and wild flowers, split the road at a tee intersection. No signs gave comforting hints to this wary traveler; no vehicles passed the lonely crossroads; the overgrown woods, dense with underbrush, seemed undisturbed by man or beast.

The road to the right headed west, followed a creek bed for a short distance, climbed the mountain, and disappeared in the glare of the early afternoon sun through the trees a quarter mile or so away. I took this road and continued for eighteen tortuous miles that took me to a paved highway back to Gainesville.

At the tee intersection two hours later, I noted the left fork continued on a downward slope to the east. I made the left turn, my only other choice. At the first bend, humiliation and shame prevailed; any harebrain would know the river lay in the valley, not on the mountaintop.

I wheeled around big bends and sharp curves, up steep grades and down gentle slopes, through hollows and over hilltops until at last I arrived. I can see it just as it was on that first visit in the summer of 1946. I see it in my mind's eye as I passed a country store—the Lost River Emporium I learned later—with the river flowing smooth and gentle on my left. Old oak trees shaded the road and fields.

I saw my first sign of life; human beings milling about in a clearing beside a big house. They waved and cheered as if at a ceremonial homecoming. I failed to understand why they gave me such a grand welcome unless to express their surprise that I actually found my way. I crossed the covered bridge that bore the only sign in the area; Lost River Bridge it read in small hand-formed letters. Before my startled eyes, I saw my father's ghost waving a red bandanna from the porch of an old house on my right.

Uncle Henry was a junior edition of my dad, ten or fifteen years younger perhaps. He wasn't a real uncle; he was a cousin removed so many times the family lost count, but you could tell the same blood ran in their veins. His home sat back from the road a hundred yards or more with the barn behind it. He stood with Aunt Lizzie and five children smiling and waving like everybody else making me feel self-conscious. The Ozark Mountain people have a reputation of hostile seclusion and pithy speech. That's their manner, I guess, but they didn't greet me that way.

Henry and Lizzie had five children. Emery, the middle of the five, was my age give or take a few months. There, the likeness stopped. He was bigger and stronger than I was. Later, I would learn shyness hid his good-humored independence with a countryboy manner, but never was I prepared for his extrasensory perception when the country boy vanished and the mystic took over.

The day after my arrival Emery walked me around the neighborhood from house to house, most of them isolated in small woodland clearings set well apart.

"Did you win any medals?"

"No. Just the routine stuff."

What a mistake! He made the same speech at every house. "My cousin served in the Canadian infantry; wounded and come home a hero; even got medals to prove it."

Try as I might, I could not make Emery understand everybody in the Canadian service routinely received medals according to where they served. The military even awarded a medal simply for voluntary enlistment. I regretted ever mentioning the subject.

We drank coffee at Applehorn's, cider at Hooper's and iced tea at somebody's home I can't remember. Between denials of military heroics, I stuffed down enough food to satisfy a platoon. At suppertime, I told Aunt Lizzie I couldn't eat another mouthful.

In the evening, I stood on the bridge abutment at the south end and dropped sticks into the river, watching them float under the bridge and disappear in the eddies. I crossed to the other end to fetch more twigs, broke them into little pieces an inch or two long and dropped them from the north end. To my amazement, they didn't flow under the bridge; they swirled in lazy circles going in the wrong direction. Dumfounded, I continued my experiments until convinced the water on the south side flowed from west to

LOST RIVER BRIDGE

east while the water on the north side moved from east to west. What was it the drummer at the boarding house said about the river flowing in two directions? And one of them uphill!

The next morning Emery took me to the river. We pushed a narrow flat-bottom square-end boat into the water. He called it a johnboat, a name I never heard before.

"Pull to the south bank below the bridge," he said, "and stop rowing." The boat bobbed down river with the gentle current.

"Pull to the other side and let her drift."

What do you know! We swung around in a circle until the bow headed upstream. Gradually the boat moved as if propelled by an unseen hand. Incredible! We floated uphill!

"How do you explain that, Emery?"

"Well, it's this way," he said. "Sometimes, when the evening sun is right, if y'all look close you'll see large fish aswimming upstream along the north bank." I leaned over to search for fish.

"No," he continued, "not today; sun's not right. Comes a time in the fall when the leaves are down and the river gets low, you can see the fins sticking out of the water."

His deadly serious face showed not the trace of a smile. I wondered just how clever these fish were. I threw a twig in. It moved in slow motion floating unnaturally the wrong way. For an instant, I thought I caught sight of a large fish, fifteen to eighteen inches, wiggling in the current with its nose pointed upstream.

"Looked like a salmon," I said, "on the way to spawn."

In the shallows on the other side, minnow-sized fish, none more than four or five inches, moved with the current downstream.

"You see, Elijah, the fish in Lost River take care of the river themselves. Coming down stream, them little fellows rest and feed. When they get to the pond at the bottom of the valley, they suck in water, much as they can hold, expanding into large fish that head upstream to the headwater. Them big wiggling fish struggling upstream makes the water flow the wrong way. At the top, they spit the water out and shrink to little fish again." His eyes roamed the surface of the river and his chin jutted forward in a startling picture of my father in serious thought.

"Gracious! For an instant you looked just like my father." He smiled and nodded. When he did not speak, I continued. "So the fish transport the water that keeps the river flowing. I suppose if they didn't do it the river would run dry and the fish would die."

"Yep," he said, stroking his chin, "reckon that's right."

"Emery! What happens if you fish the river?"

"River goes dry. When the Tabers first come here, they thought they'd found a fishing paradise. They hauled out big fish one after another. Few weeks later, the river run low. First off, everybody guessed heat was the problem. Quit fishing and after a few rains, river come back to normal. Every time they fished, it run dry. After a few years, they figured why. Nobody's fished the river since."

I rowed home pondering the mysteries of nature including the magnetic hill in Moncton, New Brunswick where cars coast uphill.

"By the way," he said as I pulled the boat ashore, "they call them fish Tankers. Ain't none others like them any place in the whole world."

I thought about that. After tying the painter to a tree, I said, "I suppose cleaning and filleting those fish created a big puddle."

"Yep," he said, gazing skyward and stroking his chin again, "reckon that's right."

I did not believe in events outside physical science and common knowledge. Unnatural phenomena were not only beyond my experience, they were beyond my belief. Cousin Emery Taber, with his masterful storytelling, casually presented them as ordinary.

Uncle Henry and Aunt Lizzie accepted me into their home with pleasant cordiality as a permanent guest, which I justified by paying room and board. My visit lasted from early July to the end of August. I stayed to further my acquaintance with Emery in an effort to understand him from my earthly perspective. I soon learned his incredible talents included conversing with ghosts and talking to ants that brought him messages from the dead.

To put it simply, I did not believe in psychics, but to this day, I remain unconvinced that his mastery of extra sensory perception was fraudulent.

Episode Two

Lost River Bridge

On my first Saturday night as a summer resident in Lost River Bridge, Aunt Lizzie organized a potluck supper to welcome me into the community. As I stepped into the meeting hall, a large portrait of a determined-looking woman overpowered me from above the stone fireplace. Her pioneer boots protruded beneath the full black skirt. Only a witty artist could capture such a bizarre detail. Sturdy hands lay folded in her lap; no rings on her fingers; no jewelry on her wrists. A white scarf draped from her shoulder hid part of a black choke collar and revealed a bold vee of pale skin above the bodice. The slight upturn of her mouth suggested a coquettish air of amusement belying the worry that lined the forehead. I read her name on the engraved plate fastened to the gold leaf frame: Sarah Agatha (Cook) Taber 1757 – 1841.

In the crowded room, a multitude of endearing souls enfolded me into their hearts. No sooner did I shake one hand than somebody dragged me off to greet a husband, hug a wife, or kiss a cousin. Taber relatives demanding attention evoked a childhood memory of an automobile trip to New England sometime in the late twenties or early thirties. I was six, or seven, or something. Soon after eight one morning in a New England town somewhere between our home in Adamsville, Quebec and Plymouth Rock, Massachusetts, Mother caught my brothers and me in a corner drugstore playing nickel slot machines. She said we must hurry. We were always in a hurry on that trip.

"Hurry, boys," she said, "today we will see the name of Philip Taber carved on a monument."

STEPHEN P. BYERS

I asked how he got away with it. If we cut our initials somewhere, or wrote our names on anything, Mother scolded us. When we arrived, I saw the name of Philip Taber all right, carved on a stone; the year 1634. I knew he didn't do it because she didn't tut-tut, perhaps because he was dead. Daddy took pictures. I threw pebbles into the sea trying to make them skip, wondering all the while about slot machines in Plymouth Rock.

Now, I stood among my Taber relatives remembering Father's frequent boasts that Philip Taber came to this country on the second Mayflower voyage. Around age ten, I gained the impression Phillip's descendants objected to the Boston Tea Party of 1773 although I had not the least idea why. A few years later I learned it curried Father's disfavor as the symbol of the breakup of our family that would not deny loyalty to the British.

Belief in friendly persuasion, and rejection of bloodshed as a means of settling disputes led my Quaker ancestors to leave New England. I belonged to the family branch known as Empire Loyalists that moved to Canada. They settled in the area now called the Eastern Townships of Quebec; a triangular region south of the Saint Lawrence River, and north of the New York-Vermont-New Hampshire border. They did not experience much change between southern Quebec and northern New England; the same weather and the same lifestyle. They built houses, barns, and raised crops. They went to prayer meetings, taught their children at home, and respected the Lord at all times.

For more than forty years, the other branch drifted through the mountains of Pennsylvania, West Virginia, and Kentucky. They shunned firearms, tried to escape the violence dominant in America, and never wrote home. The migrating Tabers moved on until they came under the leadership of a feisty woman known in the mythology of the Taber family as Granny Sarah. Her maiden name was Cook. I learned all the branches of the Taber tree, itinerant and otherwise, contended with righteous pride that she descended from Camelot although her family name suggests her ancestors may not have had a place at the Round Table. Despite Father's rambling, I never knew how Granny Sarah and her kin selected the Ozark

LOST RIVER BRIDGE

Mountains of Missouri. Maybe he didn't know either. In any event, they arrived in 1821, the year of statehood.

During the potluck supper, I sat beside Cousin Wilbur Mackay, a rotund figure with an over-inflated ego and an appetite to match. He displayed no modesty about his authority as both police and fire chief, or his reputation as self-appointed resident storyteller.

"I'd like to know the story of Granny Sarah and how she came here," I said.

When the meal ended, Wilbur rapped a spoon on the table. A few heads glanced our way, but the talk continued as loud as ever. He struggled to his feet and faced the crowd with a disgusting snort punctuated by a guttural hawk. Conversation ended. He put his handkerchief to his mouth for an instant. Then he began.

"Elijah wants to know the story of how Granny Sarah, her husband Philip, and their family come here. Well, I'm going to tell him how. Here's the way it was. A bunch of them Quakers come from Kentucky; Tabers, Harpers, Watsons, I know that for certain. Some others too maybe, but I cain't 'member no names. Anyway, they come across a man of the cloth who was right sick on the same ferry or barge or whatever it was brung them across the Mississippi. There's some what say he had a broken leg. Others say he had the fever. Whatever he had don't make no difference on account of Granny nursed him back to health. When he got better, he was much obliged to her, but she wouldn't take no money for looking after him. So he dug down in his bag and gave Granny a gold medallion of Saint Christopher. 'Course, y'all know that's the patron saint of travelers. Sarah knew she'd never have no trouble with that thing strung round her neck, so she blessed the fellow and left him to baptize the savages, or bury the outlaws, or whatever his game.

"Granny led them west over two hundred miles in the July heat until they come to a clearing in the mountains. Now, there's cool spring water bubbling out of the ground, and she figures this has to be the perfect place for her bunch to settle down and stop all this trekking. A few days later, she starts scouting around a little on account of the chiggers and ticks was pretty bad where they're camped. She takes Frieda, her oldest girl, and they go exploring in the woods. Well, you know how those things are; the insects drive them crazy and they keep going farther into the woods trying to escape. They come to a river and you can imagine how inviting it was. Off came the boots and petticoats too, I guess. Alone in the woods, you can be sure they was splashing and bathing, having a wonderful time avoiding them skeeters and gallynippers. They probably crossed to the other side, maybe on a fallen tree, or something. They wasn't paying no attention to the time, and afore they knew it the sun dipped down below the mountains, the shadows got long, and they could see the evening star. They begun searching for the way home, but Sarah realized they done a little too much playing. She knew enough to know she'd never find the way back through the wilderness in the dark."

Wilbur fascinated me with his yarn spinning. The more he talked, the more I wondered. I raised my hand to interrupt.

"Is this true, Cousin Wilbur?"

He stopped and stared at me. His jaw jutted sideways as he wiped his face on his sleeve. As his arm dropped, his fist coiled. He held it six or eight inches from my nose. I reared back. Challenging the integrity of an Ozark storyteller was an alarming experience.

"I mean, ah, it's the way you tell the story. You make it sound like you were there." I tendered a weak smile. His glowering eyes never left mine, but the fist relaxed.

"It's a legend," he growled. "Do you know what a legend is?"

"Sure," I said. "Please go on."

He began again, his gruff voice stressing the word legend, not letting me forget.

"This is the legend of the night Granny Sarah and Frieda spent in the woods. A hundred-year legend, maybe more, and I'm telling you it's as true as I'm standing here." He paused, put his hands on his hips, and glared at me for a moment.

"Now, Elijah, I don't expect you to be disbelieving like Harvey Hooper. He don't believe this story, but he's an old crank what always doubts historical records. It's 'cause he ain't a Taber and Hoopers don't have no legends, leastwise none they talk about."

LOST RIVER BRIDGE

When I looked at Harvey, I thought he was about to explode. His wife put a restraining hand on his arm. He sagged down on the bench with his elbows on the table supporting his head while the red-hot anger drained from his face. Wilbur overdid his act with a mean and nasty laugh. I could tell this wasn't the first time they feuded and I wasn't about to interfere. I waited for Wilbur to go on. Pretty soon, he hitched up his pants and continued.

"Well, there they were in the woods, Granny Sarah telling Frieda everything's going to be all right. She showed Frieda the Saint Christopher medallion. 'He was a fine Christian man,' she says, 'what looked after travelers. His job was to carry lost people over rivers and lead them home.'

"Then she says to Frieda, 'Go to sleep and it won't be long afore Jack Polecat'll come and lead us on home.'

"'Course Frieda wanted to know who this new fuddle-britches was. 'An old friend of Saint Christopher,' Granny says, 'who lives in these woods. Saint Christopher himself died years ago'.

"'Well,' says Frieda, 'when is Mr. Polecat going to show up? I'm plenty scared and want to go home.'

"Granny says, 'I got bad news for you, honey lamb, he ain't coming till morning.'

"'Gee-whiz, Mama,' says Frieda, 'you mean we're going to be here all night?'

"Now this here is the story, I mean *legend*, what Granny told.

"Once upon a time, King Arthur exiled Sir Polecat, a kind of mischievous critter who wasn't much of a knight. He told him to go build his castle in the middle of the New World. Polecat, being as how he was loyal to the King, claimed and staked the whole country, except what the Indians owned. Afore he got done building his castle, Lady Polecat up and died of homesickness. There was old Polecat stuck in the prairie for the rest of his life. When the time come for the old boy to pass on, he didn't have no heirs, obliging him to find substitutes. He called the Bobcat boys to his home.

"'Boys,' he says, 'the natives are restless and I got to do something about it. The taxes are mighty high and I think maybe the natives are planning on stealing our tea. One of you fellows is going to have to take over only I can't figure out which one. So, I'm going to have a contest. You fellows have to go out in the world and find a damsel in distress. The one what succeeds gets my job; the girl you rescue gets to be queen; and the winner takes all including inheriting the kingdom. There's just one little kicker, boys. You have to take turns, go alone and be back here in two weeks.'

"Them boys was pretty excited. They drew straws to decide who'd go first. The older cat won. He was a wonder-kid; the body of a mountain lion, the strength of an ox and the grace of a stag. More than that, he had a golden sword with a bronze shield and he rode a black stallion. I tell you this; he was a sight to make any girl's heart pound; a sure winner if you was a betting man.

"Off he goes and messes around for a week without finding a single spooked girlie. On the eighth day, he gets wind of some terrible wailing but he can't see nothing. 'I'm coming,' he shouts, riding like a buzzard with a gale for a tailwind. He rounds the bend and sees a woman in the middle of the road.

"'Tell me, little lady," he says, 'what's up?'

"When she looks at this cat her eyes flutter like a flag on a windy day. 'It ain't me,' she says, 'it's my nanny goat.'

"This comes as a big surprise to the cat and pretty much lets the air out of his bag. 'Your goat,' he says. 'What's the matter with your goat?'

She says, 'I can't milk it and I want you to help me.'

"'Look ahere, girlie,' he says, 'I'm a prince. I spent my whole life learning how to fight and be a king. I ain't milking no goat.'

"It didn't matter how much she begged, he wasn't having none of that degrading stuff. He didn't even get off his horse.

"On the ninth day, he comes across a second woman, a real lolliper as pretty as a thistle-bird. She's reaching for heaven and is bawling something fierce. The cat figures this is it. He climbs off his horse and asks this pretty gal what's going on and how come she's crowing so loud.

"She wipes her eyes and says, 'Ain't nothing the matter with me.'

LOST RIVER BRIDGE

"This puzzles the cat some so he asks, 'Why are you fussing if there ain't nothing wrong?'

"She points to a big oak and says, 'My kitten is up there and won't come down. How about you fetch her for me?'

"Now this Bobcat thinks he's the kind of fellow who hung the moon and he ain't going up no tree to catch a cat. So he turns his back, gets on his horse and off he goes without a word.

"He rode for four days looking here, there and everywhere. He was plumb wore out when he saw a huge castle so big the clouds hid the turrets. His heart went lickety-whoop and the blood flowed through his veins like water through a fire hose. He knew he'd found it this time; the home of an enormous giant. The thought of damsels in distress locked up in the dungeons just pleading for mercy got him all spurred up. Problem was he thought maybe he was near out of time, but he wasn't sure exactly.

"He knocked on the door and he banged on the door and he pounded on the door and he didn't get no answer. He flexed his muscles and stepped back twenty-eight paces. Then he charged against the door that collapsed like it was made of toothpicks. Up the stairs he went two at a time and bust into the throne room hooting and hollering he'd come to deliver a damsel from distress.

"He stopped dead. The place smelled musty and he couldn't see nothing. He drew his sword and tiptoed in the dark until way down at the far end, he seen a mousy fellow riding a hobbyhorse. The little chap has a gold crown on his head like he's the king of something.

"This here king fellow looks up and asks, 'What do you want?'

"'A damsel in distress,' says the cat.

"'Hard luck,' says the little guy. 'We ain't got none of those. Only the blessed and the blissful live here.'

"The cat figured this guy was covering up something but he decided he better check the time. He looked around and couldn't see no clock, so he asked, 'Do you have the time?'

"'Sure,' said the squirt and looked at his sundial. 'It's thirteen and a half days since you left home.'

"'You're kidding,' said the cat and his courage melted like a block of ice in hot water. 'Good gosh! I got to get home afore old Polecat disqualifies me.'

"His head hung low, his shoulders drooped. He reported his failure to Sir Polecat who kicked him out to live in the forest forever.

"The second Bobcat, who'd been lying around for two weeks grousing about his bad luck, bounced like a kid at Christmas. He faked a tear here and there while he asked his brother the details.

"Now, Bobcat Two wasn't no-wise the equal of Bobcat One. He wasn't as strong or as clever. His sword was a kind of dull silver and his shield a dirty gray metal of some kind, badly bent. On the other hand, he was one of those people that everybody loved. Folks just naturally went out of their way to help him.

"When he learned everything he could learn from his brother, Bobcat Two gathered his stuff, said goodbye and clomped from the stable on his old gray mare to find a damsel in distress. He knew exactly where the little king kept them. No use wasting time along the way on goats and pussycats. He spurred the mare past the wailing woman with the distressed goat and waved to the woman whose crazy cat thought it was a squirrel. He got to the castle two days after leaving home, dashed across the broken door and raced up the stairs to the throne room where the mousy guy with the gold crown was still riding his hobbyhorse. The little king was like everybody else. He couldn't resist this charming prince. He gave him a map of the castle. Every night the cat searched the castle and it was something else like you never seen. He found happiness overflowed from every maiden in the castle, but there wasn't one wanted to be queen. Eleven days later after non-stop parties, Bobcat Two come to breakfast at three in the afternoon to ask the time.

"The little king looked at his sundial and said, 'It's thirteen and a half days since you left home."

"'You're kidding,' said the cat and his courage melted like an ice cube in hot water. He hurried home fast as the old gray mare would go. His head hung low and his shoulders drooped. He reported his failure to Sir Polecat who kicked him out to live in the forest forever."

LOST RIVER BRIDGE

Wilbur paused and leaned his massive body toward the crowd. He scowled at the listeners indulging in an assortment of drinks and tobacco and emitting rowdy yawps of glee and contempt. His scowl quelled the crowd. Nodding heads and a chorus of groans, grunts, and growls encouraged him to continue. Or so I thought until Mr. Hooper harrumphed, waved his fist at Wilbur and said, "You, sir, ain't nothing but a no-good Taber liar."

"All right, Harvey," Wilbur said, "if you're so dang smart, you finish the legend." Harvey rose to face the audience.

"I don't know nothing about them Bobcat boys but like Wilbur says, Old Sir Polecat didn't have no children. That's the only fact in the whole legend he got right. Polecat had an adopted son name of Jack who was his only hope so he sent him off to find a wife. A good-for-nothing misfit, Jack spent his time doing chores for his stepfather and maybe them Bobcat boys, too, for all I know. They gave him an ass what Jack named Jill. She come to be his best friend. Afore leaving, he found two potatoes in the kitchen and a quarter cup of milk.

"Well, he set off down the trail and when he seen the weeping woman with the goat, he got off Jill and milked the woman's beast that was hurting pretty bad by this time. Then he rescued the cat and fed the scrawny animal the last of his milk. After he done the chores for the women, he couldn't remember for the life of him why his stepfather sent him away. Tired and hungry—he ate his last potato two days before—he lay down and fell asleep. An old witch in rags, her hair in knots, found him lying under a green apple tree. She told about a horrible bingbuffer, which, for those of you who may not know, kills by throwing stones with its hinged tail. Jack drug himself off to fight this here beast and, by golly, with his last ounce of strength, he killed it. The old witch threw her arms around him. He didn't know what to do so he kissed her. The witch turned into a beautiful princess scaring Jack half to death. He ran for his life and his freedom and that's the end of that."

Mr. Hooper shrugged. The crowd applauded and hooted. I noticed people shifting into two camps. Those on the right by the window fancied Harvey's version. The shaking heads on the left around Wilbur showed they thought even a child could not believe such rubbish. I didn't announce whose side I favored. I waited a moment trying to grasp the meaning. Before I could speak, Wilbur continued.

"Harvey you ain't finished the legend proper. When Jack refused to marry the princess, old Polecat condemned him to wander the woods forever just like the bobcats. Early one morning, Jack, wearing a beard what hung below his navel, saw a young girl with her head on her mother's lap. She smiled at him and spoke in a beautiful voice.

"'What are you doing?'

"Jack was so surprised he said he was looking for his watch, but the fact was watches wasn't invented yet. So 'course, he didn't own a watch and neither did the girl. But that didn't bother Jack none 'cause he knew someday somebody would invent one and maybe the girl had one. Anyway, watch or no watch, he wanted to know the time so he asked the girl.

"'I don't know,' she said. 'We got lost last evening and spent the whole night here by the river.'

"'That ain't no big deal,' Jack said. 'I'll take you home.'

"One at a time, he carried Granny and Frieda across the river on his shoulders. On the way back to the campsite, he mumbled it would be right smart to build a bridge over the river. When they got back to the rest of the party, everybody cheered. They thanked Jack, fed him breakfast, and praised the Lord. They figured the rescue was a promise of good fortune so they made their home by the river in the mountains of Missouri, built a crossing just like old Jack suggested and called it Lost River Bridge."

There I sat in 1946 with the descendants of Granny Sarah who considered Jack Polecat equal to Moses leading the Israelites to Canaan. All except Mr. Hooper that is, who slammed the door on his way out. As we migrated to our homes at the end of the evening, I discovered every one of my relatives and their friends swear that Jack Polecat still roams the woods around Lost River Bridge.

"As God is my witness," they say and never bat an eye.

Episode Three

Aunt Lizzie

Lost River Bridge was not a town with streets and houses jostling for space. It was an undefined and unincorporated community of isolated domains in the woods connected by twisting roads that meandered across low-water bridges and over mountain ridges. A friendly community, it radiated for miles from the river crossing. Most residents didn't know or care where their properties began and ended. They paid taxes and minded their own business. In the old days, newcomers—they're called *comeheres* in the Ozarks—squatted where they liked and waited for the County to find them. Times have changed; it's been more than fifty years since the last settler squatted in Lost River Bridge. These days the land is bought and sold like everywhere else with the records kept in the County Office in Gainesville. The most remote residents lived five or six miles off the main road. No signs pointed to the beginning or end of town. Just a backwoods region in the mountains of Ozark County overlooked and unrecorded by all except the County Assessor.

The center of this cluster of mountain folk was a large house known as The Applehorn Place in a clearing to the east of the bridge on the north side. Across the road, a decrepit log building served as a meeting hall and community center. Standing on the road in front of Applehorn's, I could see the Lost River Emporium a quarter mile away; a log building more than a hundred years old. Through the trees across the river, I glimpsed Henry and Lizzie's home with its tarpaper patches over the imitation brick siding and asbestos shingles. Otherwise, I saw no sign of civilization. A stranger stopping at the bridge would never know he stood in the midst of a miracle; a community resurrected from the depths of degradation.

I heard appalling tales about Ozark mountaineers eking out a livelihood hidden in the forests of the American hinterland prior to the Civil War. An insular society of independent frontiersmen had more respect for their horses and guns than their women and children. They clawed nourishment from the forest in the form of possum, squirrel, rabbit, and deer; made moonshine whiskey; grew crops in the rock-hard soil; and snatched a living from the land. Unsanitary conditions and frequent childbearing brought disease and sometimes early death to women who faced constant scrubbing, endless cooking, and lustful demands of husbands gone who knows where for months at a time. The reconstruction period after the Civil War brought even greater danger; roving bands of lawless, homeless men. Nondescript clusters of isolated communities populated to a large degree by widows, children, and old folks could do little to defend themselves against the marauders, and the hard times.

Then, a miracle revitalized life in Lost River Bridge; Abner Applehorn came to live there. Single-handedly, he uplifted the community restoring pride and decency. Until the influx of automobiles in the second decade of the twentieth century, and rural electrification made radio possible a few decades later, Abner delivered inspiration like a savior bringing spiritual renewal. In the twenties and thirties the outside world, with new mobility and quickening technology, discovered these modest mountain people, and declared them archaic eccentrics. I loved them all.

Henry's house faced east. The sun climbed above the mountaintop reminding the rooster to beam its wake-up call between six and seven each morning; that is when it wasn't raining. In the summertime, Lizzie and Henry ate their breakfast on the porch and waved to the neighbors. Because they lived on the road leading to the bridge, the only artery crossing Lost River, most anybody going anywhere passed by their place. A year or two after they built the house, Lizzie said she'd like to enjoy the sunset as well. Henry obliged by building a stone patio at the rear. He rescued a rusty ta-

LOST RIVER BRIDGE

ble with a red and blue Cinzano umbrella, and four antique chairs from a dump somewhere. When Aunt Lizzie finished making upholstered grain-bag cushions, they were comfortable if a little prickly. So it was, during my summer visit, I ate Aunt Lizzie's grits and hominy in the morning sunshine, and homemade pies beneath a tattered sunshade in the evening. I listened to family stories that began at dawn, and ended as the sun drew the nighttime curtain across the sky.

"Tell me, Emery, how is it your mother has that nickname?"
"She don't have any."
"You mean her real name isn't Elizabeth?"
This is the story he told about the baptism of Lizzie Applehorn.

"Mama's the youngest daughter of my grandpa, Abner Applehorn. He come to these parts about 1880. Folks used to say tragedy brought him to the Ozark Mountains. You know how folks are always making up stories 'bout what they don't know. There's some what said he'd killed a man; others whispered about a death in the family. Papa said he heard a fellow say one time Grandpa robbed a bank and escaped from jail. Ain't none of them stories true.

"Truth is he come from German ancestry. His father's name was Affels something, or whatever the German word for apples. Born in America, he done his schooling in English. When he growed up, he didn't want to be no beer-making German like his papa. He left home, changed his name, and settled here."

I hadn't forgotten the reproof from Wilbur for interrupting his story, but I couldn't resist a comment. "Seems curious to me why a fellow like that would come here in the first place."

Emery turned his head sideways. It was easy to see I was in for another scolding. He paused and took a deep breath. "Elijah," he said, "you ain't got no imagination."

"I guess not."
"Cain't you guess?"
I confess I admired the way he made me feel so stupid, but I had no idea. I offered a helpless shrug.

"'Cause of Effy Harper. What other reason makes a man move from here to there?"

"I should have known. Go on."

"Abner took up cattle and dairy farming; expanded into chickens, sheep, goats, and horses; built a barn and silo down in the Bryant River valley. Yes, sir, he become the biggest rancher these parts ever knowed. He'd tell folks he never had no money. Lots of it passed through his fingers, all of it spent on farm animals and children. Folks was always asking if he loved his animals or his kids more. Except only one time, he never bought anything for hisself. In forty years, he become a rich man; richest man in Ozark County, they say. I'd guess he inherited money from his beer-making daddy, too. About 1910, he built the big house on the other side of the river; big enough for three of his children and their families to live in it today.

"A year or two after the turn of the century, Grandpa saw an automobile for the first time. That car haunted him night and day. When he couldn't stand it no more, he went on up to Springfield to see 'bout buying one.

"'Three hundred and sixty-nine dollars,' the salesman said.

"It happened Abner'd spent everything he could afford for something on the farm; probably more animals. Besides that, he thought spending that much money on a contraption for hisself what was nothing, but a toy was kind of selfish; that's the sort of man he was. He tried to forget 'bout the car, but he couldn't. Granny Effy didn't help none, either.

"'Why Abner,' she said, 'you go ahead and buy that machine. You never do nothing for yourself; it's always the children, the animals, and me.'

"They talked 'bout it for a whole year. Finally, he allowed he'd start a savings program, and when he had enough money, he'd buy a car. I can imagine Grandpa Abner standing in front of the salesman, hat pushed back, scratching his head, and asking, 'Got anything cheaper?' He didn't buy nothing he didn't bargain for.

"'Not right now, but perhaps I can find a second-hand one.'

"'You don't say.' Grandpa couldn't hide his interest. 'How much?'

"'Maybe a hundred, hundred fifty perhaps. The bank will lend money on your home or farm. You'd be better off to go ahead and take the new one.'

"'Sure am tempted,' Abner said, 'but no, there ain't no way. I never owed anybody for anything in my life, and I ain't going to start now. No Sir! I'll save till I got enough to pay for it full; then I'll buy.'

"Abner begun to save his nickels and dimes in a glass carboy hid in the corner of the bedroom. Effy attached a label that said "Abner's Car." It was a family game; children dropping pennies and nickels in then dumping it out every Saturday night at bath time to count it. The jar filled up pretty quick. So much so, it surprised the lot of them. Grandpa didn't say nothing, but I'd guess he dumped in most of the cash when there weren't no one looking. He always said he never done that, but most folks think he did. In the end, it turned out the children learned a lesson 'cause every one of them come to be tight-fisted misers, including Mama, and she weren't even born yet. Anyway, in the springtime, it took two or three them kids to lift it. They finally counted one hundred and twenty-five dollars, and they clamored to go with him to Springfield. 'Course, none had ever seen a car; didn't know what one looked like. That was when Granny came to him, put her arms around his neck, and whispered in his ear.

"'Going to have another baby.'

"The news delighted Abner. He loved his big family; had a soft spot in his heart for every one of them especially the girls. He and Effy agreed when they got married she'd name each boy child, and he'd pick the name if the baby was a girl.

"When the time neared for Granny Effy to deliver, she begun having strange pains. She'd had six children and knew them pains wasn't the usual ones.

"'I'll not buy a car until after the new baby comes,' Abner said to his kids. He wouldn't leave her for even a minute. 'Just wait,' he said. 'Few more weeks and we'll buy our first car, but your mother's health, and the baby come first.'

"Early one morning Effy came to him looking miserable. 'Something's wrong, Abner,' she said.

"'What's the trouble?'

"'I've brung six children into this world, but I ain't never felt like this afore.'

"The nearest doctor was down to Mountain Home in Arkansas. The mid-wife didn't know what to do. Abner couldn't hardly stand to see Effy suffer. He had to do something. So he set a mattress in the carriage, told the mid-wife to come with them, and he took Effy for the long ride to the doctor who sent her right smack into bed.

"'You better go on home, Abner, and look after your young ones,' the doctor said. 'I'm going to keep Effy here. Maybe I'll have to take her to the hospital, but don't you worry none, I'll look after her right well.'

"In the end, everything turned out fine. Effy recovered after delivering a baby girl to the Applehorn family. A few weeks later when she came home, she had something else. She handed Abner a bill for one hundred twenty-five dollars for the special nurses, the medicines, five weeks room and board, and who knows what else.

"Abner threw a fit, stomped on his hat and screamed. 'A hundred twenty-five dollars! We never paid no more than ten dollars for a baby before. I can't pay a hundred and twenty-five dollars. I don't make that much money in a year.'

"Effy just looked at him and smiled 'cause she knew about the automobile money. 'What would you rather have, Abner, an automobile or a baby?'

"Abner looked at her with his head kind of sideways like. 'I'll have to think about that,' he said. He set there for a while with his arms folded across his chest. Suddenly, he looked up to face her. 'No. I don't have to think about that. We have a house full of children. I pick the automobile.'

"Effy's mouth dropped open like she was hit on the head with a betsey. The fight begun, and didn't stop for weeks. Abner moved on out to the farm so as to avoid the argument at home. He said he had to tend sick animals. With him away not paying no never mind,

LOST RIVER BRIDGE

Effy took the jar from the bedroom, went to the Gainesville bank, and sent the money to the doctor. When Abner came home to attend church the following Sunday, one of the children whispered in his ear. Sure enough, he found the jar empty. Effy 'fessed up. He wouldn't talk to her. They went to church, sat through the service, and walked home never saying one single word one to the other. That night, he ate his supper and went to bed without a word to Effy. She ignored his fussing.

"'What you going to name the baby?'

"He didn't answer.

"Effy had enough of this nonsense. The next Sunday when the preacher come to town, she arranged for the baptizing. She come home and told Abner about it. 'Preacher's going to baptize the baby next Sunday. You better pick a name or I'm going to do it for you, and that's all there is to that.' She left him brooding at the table like a hungry mule at an empty trough.

"Well, there they were on Sunday morning, Abner, Effy, six children, and a babe in arms crowding the front pew. Abner paid no never mind to the service. He sulked, all upset 'cause Effy broke the family rules. He had the right to name the girls and arrange the baptism. She'd done it without asking. On second thought, maybe she did ask. Did she or didn't she? He couldn't remember anything. You know sometimes how it is you just can't think, like there's a fog covering your memory. He looked at the baby, shook his head, and closed his eyes. Pictures of the car—the first car to drive the roads of Lost River Bridge—was all he could see. The preacher mumbled the usual stuff while Abner shifted into a world of his own. He soared out of the church, past the cemetery, and across the bridge in his finest Sunday outfit, new hat and all, zipping along at ten miles an hour in search of a name, never to hitch another team.

"The preacher smiled and took the little baby into his arms. 'In the name of the Father and the Son and the Holy Ghost I name this child ... .'

"Silence fell. Everybody in the whole church pushed forward waiting to hear the name. Preacher glared at Abner, whose head nodded back and forth, eyes shut. Pastor shifted his gaze to Effy.

She set there, her jaw stiff, face red, and lips drawn tight.
"Suddenly, she drove her elbow into Abner's ribs. 'Name her!'
"Abner was in the middle of the prairie somewhere with the countryside swishing past lickety-whoop. What was he going to name his first automobile? He gasped and squealed like a hog.
"'Oooh! Tin Lizzie!'
"The pastor's brow furrowed, his eyes opened wide and he stared at Abner. At last, he mumbled, 'Old Tin Lizzie.'
"After the service, the pastor shook Abner's hand.
"'That sure is an unusual name you give that child, Abner. How do you spell that? I have to write it in the registry.'
"'I ain't rightly sure,' Abner said, turning his face away, 'but I reckon it's A-L-T-E-N.' He paused, but there weren't nothing else come to his mind so he said, 'L-I-Z-Z-I-E.'
"The pastor laid the baby in Abner's arms. A little hand reached out and a tiny fist grasped Abner's index finger. He turned to Effy.
"'She likes that name,' he said. 'I think she smiled at me. She's going to be a laugher.' His eyes glowed with kind of sheepish grin on his face. 'I can tell. She likes jokes.'

He paused looking down at Baby Lizzie. Some folks in church that day said as what they thought he was telling her he was sorry for what he'd done; but not me. I'm mighty sure he was athinking hard on what to say to Effy. At last, he looked up and took ahold of Effy's hand. 'I guess I'd rather have the baby,' he said.

Episode Four

The Pursey Boys

A mile west of the bridge, in a hollow beyond the hill, sat The First Methodist Church. On our way to service one Sunday, Uncle Henry told me the history of the church. The Society of Friends Meeting House stood on the site for about fifty years. Sometime in the first half of the nineteenth century, most of the Quakers had died, or moved on. The Southern Baptists took over, but the building burned to the ground soon after. In 1860, a new church rose on the same site with Methodist affiliation. Elijah Pursey, the first resident preacher in the community, returned from college in Pennsylvania importing the philosophy of John Wesley.

"Did the denominational changes bother anybody, Uncle Henry?"

He stopped to glare at me. I had become aware of the sensitivity of mountain people to questions that might reflect on the integrity of their stories. He pushed his hat to the back of his head and appeared bewildered before he answered.

"Why ask a question like that?"

"Well, I thought that maybe—"

He put his hands on his hips and sneered at me with a curious expression. "Only one God, ain't there? What difference does it make what you call the church?"

I shrugged and dropped the subject. As we walked on, I learned Elijah never locked the doors to his church. The Catholics in the area used it regularly. After Elijah died, the Catholics built their own church outside Lost River Bridge on the way to Gainesville.

STEPHEN P. BYERS

Walking home after service, Uncle Henry talked about the cemetery. When the plot between the church and the river couldn't hold more graves, the townsfolk consecrated a new burial ground across the road. Based on the death rate and the community expansion, they calculated the space they needed, then multiplied by five to make sure. They fenced the four-acre plot, but only cleared a small portion leaving the rest for future generations. The iron entrance gate bore the name Sarah Taber Memorial Cemetery. Somebody offered a proposal at the annual cemetery meeting to move Granny Sarah to the new site. They've been considering it for about fifty years now, but have not settled the matter. In undisturbed glory, Sarah continues to rest at the top of the hill behind the church.

Uncle Henry suggested I work with Emery the next day mowing and weeding the cemetery. Since the age of fifteen, Emery has been caretaker of the church. By ten o'clock in the morning, my Canadian blood found the ninety-five degree heat unbearable. I stopped to rest every few minutes. The temperature didn't seem to bother Emery, but when I stopped, he didn't hesitate to collapse beside me.

He had a habit of rubbing one hand on the grass as if feeling for a lost article. When an ant climbed his finger, he lifted his hand close to his mouth and talked to the creature. He asked about the cemetery news; about the colony affairs and if they had enough food. Between questions, he'd pause with his head cocked sideways. Presently, he set it on the grass. I sensed an idea brewing in his mind and judged the ant act as a search for a way to express it. He surprised me when he began.

"In the old Ozark days, mountain folks didn't have much money. Without no money, lots of stealing and robbing and stuff like that went on. Wasn't much to look forward to except dying. What they done to escape was make moonshine. Outsiders didn't want to live in the hills with folks drinking all the time, firing guns and stealing whatever they could. That's what caused inbreeding among the family groups scattered in the mountains. It wasn't like that in Lost River Bridge because new families kept coming here."

LOST RIVER BRIDGE

He mumbled almost under his breath, his head nodding in the manner of my father as if trying to convince himself rather than me. "Yeah, lots of them come to Lost River Bridge. For over a hundred years maybe."

He wiped his mouth on his short-sleeve shirt, tugged his tobacco from the breast pocket of his overalls, rolled a cigarette and passed the makings to me. After a couple of puffs and blowing the smoke skyward to watch it drift away on the gentle breeze, he continued.

"My daddy says they come 'cause Granny Sarah made it a place where people liked to live."

He took a deep drag and expelled the smoke with an audible sigh. I felt time linger with each pause and wanted to urge him on, but I held my tongue. Another moment of thought; then he spoke again.

"I guess maybe that's partly true, but I think most come just 'cause folks here didn't shoot and rob one another. Sure they was stills, but not that many. The church didn't like them and most everybody here is religious and goes to church on Sunday. But I ain't sure." He pursed his lips and nodded his head exactly like my father. "Me! I think it was good luck and nothing else." His head nodded and again I saw my father agreeing with himself. He hit his fist into his hand and grimaced like the preacher stressing the gospel. "That's right. Just good luck! 'Course, comeheres don't always make good citizens, but the spirit of Christianity in Lost River Bridge welcomes everyone. That's what saved them from themselves."

His southern drawl, punctuated with long pauses, invoked the image of a slow-witted country boy. In the end, he made his point well and I questioned my assessment. I wondered if he developed these ideas on his own or repeated a theory he heard elsewhere. I didn't ask and he fell to telling a tale that I suppose he intended as proof. Here it is in my words, not his.

About the time Granny Sarah arrived in the Ozarks, the Pursey brothers, Mark and Luke, settled on the Missouri prairie with their parents and younger brother and sister. Their father charged them with the responsibility of putting meat on the table, allowing him to stay home to protect his family and care for the crops. The two boys returned from a weeklong hunt to find their parents and siblings massacred, their home burned to the ground. Mark and Luke moved away from the prairie. About 1825, they straggled into Lost River Bridge and told their story to Granny Sarah. She welcomed them thinking, no doubt, about prospective husbands for her unmarried daughters.

In four years, the industrious Tabers cleared land, built houses and barns, bought farm animals, and found time to erect a Meeting House for Sunday prayer. Mark and Luke became enthusiastic contributors and welcome suitors for eligible daughters.

A romance developed between Luke and Rebecca, Sarah's second daughter. The next spring, Luke came home with Rebecca on a Sunday after church service. She quietly vanished leaving the poor boy stammering his intentions to Granny Sarah and her husband, Philip. Sarah recruited every available female to organize the first wedding in the Taber family since they arrived in Missouri. Philip and his neighbors built a traditional Ozark home for the soon to be newlyweds; two rooms separated by a dogtrot. The wedding of Luke Pursey and Rebecca Taber, so painstakingly planned and lovingly sponsored, became an unexpected nightmare for Granny Sarah brought about by the arrant jealousy of the oldest daughter Frieda.

Mark, more aggressive than his younger brother, did not accept the binding customs of the Quakers. He set about to exercise friendly persuasion on long Sunday afternoons tromping across the meadows with Frieda. He preached a different interpretation than the philosophy of the church. Slowly, Frieda's resistance crumbled until, when she learned of Rebecca's engagement, it vanished. That evening, her fresh and vigorous cheeks told the story. She confessed to Rebecca. Three days before the wedding, Sarah took Rebecca aside to advise her about the expectations of the wedding night. Without thinking, Rebecca blurted out, "Yes, I know Mother. Frieda told me about it."

LOST RIVER BRIDGE

The common characteristic of Quakers—leastwise the Taber Quakers a hundred years ago—was the ability to put on the cloak of stoicism. It is impossible to equal them in the category of martyrdom. Sarah put on the mantle, prepared to accept death rather than Frieda's sin. She refused to reveal, even to her husband, the mortification that enveloped her. The worst blow, however, was yet to come. In a fit of rage on the morning of the wedding, Frieda told her mother she was pregnant. Sarah climbed into a pious cocoon and retired to her bed for three days immediately after the nuptials. In direct confrontation with Philip and Sarah several weeks later, Mark refused to marry. Without explanation to the community, they banished Frieda from their home. Mark, having lost his brother to Rebecca and his sweetheart to exile, left for parts unknown.

Frieda found lodging and employment in Gainesville. Sarah had taught her well. She became an instant success as a seamstress making bonnets, aprons and accessories for women. Her products brought local fame and demand for more elaborate articles. She branched into scarves, hankies and sachets. The bonanza arrived when she agreed to mend a pair of unmentionables in a whispered conversation. The whisper echoed through the afternoon teas and quilting bees until Frieda had to refuse to undertake more orders. She wrote to her mother not only to boast of success, but also to say the baby was due in two weeks and she wished her mother would be with her. And so we come to the second Taber quality. Still not recovered from the shock of her unrepentant daughter's pregnancy, nonetheless Sarah set her martyr's cloak aside and did her duty.

Frieda, suffering first from morning sickness and later from overwork, existed in Gainesville in her own world unaware of the social environment or the snickering gossip. She met many women, but did not develop close friendships, paying little heed to what was going on around her. She failed to notice a blacksmith named Cassias Morton. She was, in fact, unaware of his existence. On the other side of town, he was aware of her, but could not muster the courage to make his interest known. Her pregnancy did not concern him. In fact, he considered it an equalizer for he was the father of a two-year old boy who lived with his grandmother. The boy's mother died in childbirth. When news circulated that Frieda produced a baby boy, Cassias read it as a sign from the Lord. Being illiterate, he asked his mother to write a letter wishing Frieda good fortune and good health. Eight months later, Cassias and Frieda married.

The marriage relieved Sarah's troubled heart. She urged them to live in Lost River Bridge, but Frieda, having witnessed her mother's behavior for so many years, put on her own cloak of martyrdom. She justified her exile by accusing her mother of various faults, real and imaginary. What a glorious relationship! Who could ask for a better affinity between a Taber mother and a Taber daughter. To indulge martyrdom brought a degree of righteousness that became dinnertime conversation in their separate homes. The best part was making the sacrifice to do one's duty by visiting and complaining bitterly afterwards. One or other, but never the two at the same time, could always find solace through sacrifice by setting aside stoic reflections and performing her duty.

All this I learned under the shade of an oak tree for two hours while we smoked three cigarettes each. I sensed our rest period ending. I asked a question.

"How do you know all this stuff?"

Emery looked at me with unblinking eyes, his mouth slightly ajar. I still had not learned that storytelling is a cottage industry in the Ozarks. I obviously insulted him. At last he spoke.

"What do you mean?"

"Nothing. I mean this tale took place about a hundred and twenty years ago. I have no idea what happened to my relatives that long ago. How come you know all these details?"

My explanation did not relieve his irritation. He folded himself back to his knees and resumed weeding without a word.

"Listen, Emery! I'm sorry. I didn't mean to hurt your feelings. I'm just curious how you know what you've been telling me."

He did not look up from his work.

LOST RIVER BRIDGE

"You don't believe me."

My inclination was to say that's right, but I caught myself in time. I thought it best to carry on with my chores so I clambered to my knees beside him and said nothing. We worked in silence for perhaps ten minutes.

"It's true," he said.

"I'm sure it is."

"You don't believe me."

"Emery! Let's not go through this again. I said I believe you. More than that, I'd like to hear the end of the story."

He jumped to his feet. "Come here!"

I followed up the gentle slope to the highest spot in the old cemetery behind the church. A huge oak tree shaded the ground.

"There," he said.

He pointed at two graves side by side. Most monuments seemed randomly placed in more or less straight lines, but these two stood apart from the others. I dropped to my knees to read the inscriptions on weathered slab markers. One was Sarah Taber; the other Frieda Morton who died eleven years before her mother.

"Well," I said. "What happened?"

"Frieda had two more children. She died a year after the last one was born." His voice was soft in the slight breeze rustling the leaves. "Granny Sarah loved Frieda more than any other child."

Emery stood beside me, his unblinking eyes fixed in space. The strange mask contorting his face gave me the eerie feeling he could see the two women. When he spoke his remark did not address me. His words sailed into space like the smoke from his cigarette. I didn't exist in the world he shared with his two ancestors.

"Of course you loved her, Granny. What else could explain how badly you treated each other if not love?"

He turned to me.

"They buried Frieda here 'cause Granny Sarah said to bury her here. Before the casket closed, Granny put a gold Saint Christopher medallion in Frieda's hand. 'When my time comes,' she said, 'I want to be buried close to Frieda so Saint Christopher will carry us safely home again.'"

Episode Five

Making Money

In the evenings, I sat in the yard behind the house with Emery and his brothers and sisters. They seemed intent on testing my credulity. Even the youngest told stories about twenty-two-foot snakes seen with his own eyes, and three-hundred-pound catfish thrown back because they were too small. They spoke of cougar fish that caused boating accidents. Despite large rewards for their extermination, no one has ever caught a cougar fish. I learned side-hill-dodgers have two short legs on the uphill side. On meeting one of these fearsome beasts, they advised withdrawal in a downhill circle until the animal, which will always follow the retreat, topples harmlessly away. The most famous Ozark creatures are gowrows. They live in the mountains, and seldom come out except to fish with trolls under bridges. They dine only on young children, usually after dark when disobedient youngsters stay up too late, and sometimes when they make too much noise and scare the fish.

One evening when Uncle Henry joined us, I noticed smoke rising above the trees.

"Looks like a fire over there," I said.

His response puzzled me. He gazed into the distance while a smile creased his face.

"Don't see nothing," he said.

He wasn't looking in the direction I pointed. With unconcerned nonchalance, he ignored my comment. Another lesson about Ozark ways; if they don't want you to know something, you can ask forever, but you will never get an answer. Overcome with sudden deafness, Uncle Henry launched into an unrelated tale. Maybe it dated from the old days when revenuers asked about stills.

The deliberate evasion stirred my curiosity. Venturing off on my own in search of the smoke source would be foolish. I knew neither the path nor the distance. Getting lost was not only dangerous, but they might leave me to wander the woods forever like Jack Polecat. Perhaps I could pry the information from Emery. The next day, I went with him to the cemetery.

"Oh sure," he said, "you could walk there. Ain't much to see. Sawmill closed down a while back. Belongs to the Bellechase family. His grandsons own it now."

"Sawmill? You sure it's not a still?" A bold guess on my part.

"Was. His grandsons turned it into a sawmill a few years after prohibition ended. We could take your car, but the road ain't been used for a while; probably rough."

"How rough?"

After a long pause, he shrugged and grimaced. His head swiveled towards Granny Sarah's grave. He drifted into a hypnotic state with unblinking eyes. I held my tongue in fascination at this astonishing ritual of calling the deceased at will. A shiver ran through his body suspending him in time like the instant before a sneeze.

"Granny says we should walk."

Who was I to challenge Granny's wisdom?

"Let's go tomorrow," I said.

We marched through the woods on a road that would break the axle of a Mack truck, never mind my old Studebaker. The sun beat down, but fortunately we walked in shade most of the way. I peeled off my shirt to swat at the buzzing insects. At first, Emery appeared immune to the discomfort until I realized the perspiration dripping from his face and soaking his shirt camouflaged a singular anguish and disinclination to talk. I tried a question in the hope of raising his spirit.

"How did old Bellechase get his supplies in here?"

Thirty or forty paces later, he mumbled a response.

"Brung 'em up the river, I guess."

I took a few more stabs at conversation asking about trees, wild animals, gowrows, anything that crossed my mind. He dismissed my efforts with terse replies and martyred grunts. More than two hours after our start, we arrived at a clearing overgrown with weeds. Abandoned equipment littered the property as if the workers left one evening expecting to come back, but never returned. A decayed lean-to with rusty galvanized metal siding creaked and moaned in the wind, creating an eerie sensation. I stared in fascination with an alert nervousness I couldn't explain. Emery perched on the blade of a rusty bulldozer and drank from his thermos. He passed it to me and rolled a cigarette with one hand while I slaked my thirst. I capped the bottle and let my eye examine the decrepit building from bottom to top. About mid-way across the roof, I saw two sheets of new galvanized iron glistening in the sun.

"Emery, how did those two new sheets of tin get up there?"

His eyes roamed over the metal surface. Without a word, he pushed himself to his feet and disappeared around the end of the building. In a few moments, he reappeared at the opposite end.

"Got some new pieces on the walls round back," he said as he kicked the siding.

I think I saw the flash before I heard the report, but they came so close together they were simultaneous. The bullet struck a hard surface somewhere. Impelled by instinct, I reacted to the whine of the ricochet I had heard so often in Europe, but I felt like I moved in slow motion. I cowered behind the blade of the bulldozer, unable to think. I raised my head; Emery stood with his hands on his hips, a look of bewilderment, rather than surprise, on his face.

"Get Down! Emery! Get down behind the truck!"

He looked at me. His expression changed to one of incomprehension. His heart murmur precluded service in the military, and he had no notion what to do in a surprise attack. Or, so I thought.

"Emery! Listen to me. Lie down!"

I crept towards him protected by the steel blade. He did not move. I could see his eyes scanning the building. Then he spoke for the first time since the gunshot.

"Ah ha!" His voice was gruff, raspier than I ever imagined it could be. It brought to mind Sergeant Martin who delighted in mak-

LOST RIVER BRIDGE

ing my European sojourn as miserable as he could.

Emery strode towards the building. I looked in the direction he walked and saw the barrel of a rifle protruding through the metal siding. He paid no attention to my warning shout. I had no choice. Running a zigzag pattern, I tried to tackle him. He pushed me to the ground with his left hand like a football halfback. His right hand grabbed the rifle barrel.

"Get out of there," he ordered in his Sergeant Martin voice. He tugged on the rifle with two hands. I cringed as he pulled the muzzle against his belly. The corner of the sheet metal bent; the weapon came loose. From where I lay on the ground, it looked like a Lee-Enfield three-oh-three. A moment later the shed door squeaked open. Two men emerged, mid-forties, perhaps, hands held high above their heads.

I lead a five-man patrol through a copse three hundred yards in front of Company A. We make no noise except the soft crunch of our boots. To my right, I glimpse the back of three German helmets projecting an inch or two above ground. Their backs are to me. I point. My patrol drops to the ground. They take aim and wait for my order. I check the magazine on my automatic, stand with my feet astride, my finger on the trigger.

"Achtung!"

Three heads jerk around. I am close enough to see fear in their eyes. Their hands go above the heads. I want to laugh. Each man holds a half-eaten loaf of dark-brown bread. Waving the muzzle of my gun, I direct them to emerge. They clamber from the trench without weapons and stare at us with hands still high in the air clutching their bread. One of them glances over his shoulder.

"It's a trap!"

I hit the ground looking for the Trojan Horse that will disgorge the enemy. I see them with my unbelieving eyes rising from foxholes amid the trees. They look more like timid prairie dogs than Hector's Trojan warriors. Some carry weapons pointed skyward, most have potato masher grenades hanging from their belts, all have backpacks, and every single last one has his hands above his head holding a loaf of brown bread.

"They've quit, boys! They're surrendering! They don't want to fight no more!"

I take a deep breath trying to slow my heartbeat.

"Hank! Get Sergeant Martin. Tell him we need help! The rest of you take their weapons. Line these guys up, and no looting."

I examine the prisoners; twenty-two dispirited men who have heiled their last heil. A corporal leads them; a corporal just like me only he isn't like me—he's forty-five years old if a day. All of them are sullen, unshaven fathers admitting the futility of a war they don't want to fight. They put their families above loyalty to country. Their war is over.

"Hey, Sarge! They ain't got no officer. Think one of them guys killed him?

"Elijah!"

I scrambled to my feet with a mortifying gawk unable to dispel the image of Emery grasping the rifle. In ten months in the European Theater, I never saw anybody walk into the face of a sniper as he did that day. I was too astounded to ask if he was stupid or fearless, but there he stood in the door to the shed, alive.

"What are you doing?"

"Just . . . nothing," I said.

"Come here and look at this."

An antiquated machine long past any conceivable use stood in the center of the shed. Rough board siding of the sort one sees on decayed barns enclosed the contraption. On one side, it had a steel-rimmed wagon wheel with handholds around the perimeter in the fashion of a navigation wheel on a sea-going ship. A hand lever from an old steam engine projected from the opposite side. It measured about two feet by five; a relic no self-respecting museum would ever display.

"What is it?"

"Armand Côté made it around 1900. These fellows are his sons. They just bought this place from the Bellechase boys."

The two men standing in the dark shadows looked to be of

LOST RIVER BRIDGE

French-Canadian extraction like those I knew at home in Quebec. When I spoke in French, they looked at each other in bewilderment.

One of them stepped forward, offering his hand. "Sorry, we don't speak French."

I reached for his hand and held it tight in both of mine. I didn't care where they came from or who they were.

"How come you guys shot at us?"

"We didn't know who you were."

"Oh! Come on. Don't give me that stuff."

"We wanted to scare you off, that's all."

Emery stepped between us. I let go and moved back.

"Elijah, you just ain't use to mountain ways."

Emery accepted the incident with a smile and no questions, which allowed me to understand his behavior under fire. The two men tried to soothe my jangled nerves by offering a drink.

"Drink of what?"

"Whiskey."

"Not me. Come on, Emery, let's go."

Emery pulled a chair from beside a table and sat.

"Elijah! Get off your high horse. We didn't walk here just so we could walk back. We ain't going until we hear their story. Sit down"

I smiled, sat, and shook my head.

"I should have known a story came in the same package. Go ahead! Let's hear it." Here it is in my words.

Despite being a talented sculptor and carver, nobody recognized the artistic ability of Armand Côté in his native Quebec. Unable to provide for his family, he and Henri Bellechase, Lucien's son, became a traveling craft show. They wanted to be voyageurs, but the railroads had come and transportation by canoe was dead. Instead, they left home in the early spring and returned in the late fall. Paddling and portaging canoes along the old voyageur's routes, they peddled Armand's artwork. After trying a bunch of alternatives, Armand hit on metal engraving as something he could do in the evenings when the long days ended. The hand tools and small work objects didn't need much space and added little to the weight of his backpack. His religious artifacts brought a handsome return. Creating souvenirs from money was the simplest and fastest of all tasks. A five-cent coin he imprinted in a few minutes sold for five times face value. The higher the denomination, the greater the profit. In a moment of inspiration, he copied a dollar bill on a rigid master plate. Placing a thin strip of metal over the template and rubbing with a stone, he achieved an acceptable souvenir that brought even greater monetary rewards. That was the turning point.

Two years later they abandoned their game and returned to Lost River Bridge to distill whiskey. It was there that Armand built this machine and fed his counterfeit money into the commercial stream. The venture met with unimaginable success.

Old Lucien, Henri's father, selected the location expressly because of the water. A clear spring fed a small tributary of Lost River. He bought his grain supplies at various sites along the White and Bryant Rivers, moved them by canoe to a secluded cove three miles from the still. From there, he lugged fifty-pound sacks while walking in the streambed to baffle the revenuer's bloodhounds. The newly arrived ex-peddlers fell into the same routine, reinvigorating the still and achieving local fame as respected entrepreneurs.

Armand realized that most business involved small denomination coins whereas he produced paper money up to twenty-dollar bills. He engraved dies to produce coinage, built a press and entered competition with the US Mint. The Revenuers found his efforts far more disturbing than distillation of whiskey. An ever-increasing force of agents searched the Midwest. An agent got his hands on a seven-dollar bill Armand put into circulation in the belief it would be a convenient unit of currency. At the Lost River Emporium, the agent bought a small article for thirty cents. He casually offered the illegal bill. With equal composure, the clerk rang the register and handed him the change. He held two three-dollar bills and two thirty-five cent pieces.

Armand squirreled away enough legitimate money for his family to live comfortably. In jail, he reverted to carving and sculpting with carefree contempt for the tiny income they produced.

Episode Six

Elijah T. Pursey

The lack of specific knowledge does not deter the Ozark storyteller who relates with unabashed sincerity an event from firsthand personal experience seen with his own eyes, sometimes even if the event happened years before his birth. Often, the response to a good tale is a longer, greater or more unusual event that occurred at some other time or place. Thus, sighted snakes grow continually longer and rejected catfish unceasingly heavier.

I discovered luring tellers into one-on-one solo performances avoided arguments about misinformation offered by other tellers, leaving me free to make my own determination to accept or reject. Thus, I set out to learn the story of Elijah Taber Pursey, one storyteller at a time. I uncovered mysticism surrounding Reverend Pursey in the tales about his bond with the Lord. Some suggested he communed directly with God. Others reversed the communion, believing God talked to Elijah as He did to the Old Testament prophet. Elijah looked the part of the prophet in Uncle Henry's tintype reproduction that showed an image that fit the description; scraggy beard stretching a pious face under a traditional Quaker *wide-awake* hat. He wore a cape in the picture that put me in mind of his namesake striding into battle against the forces of Baal.

After church service, I walked home with Lou Pursey avoiding as best I could the stench of strong drink seasoned with cut plug tobacco. Born ten years before me, he served six years in the US navy. Unmarried and lonely, he earned his keep working his father's land while living with his sister and her family in the house their father built in 1922. Most nights he drank his supper and staggered out to the fields next day to sweat it out.

"Elijah Taber Pursey was your great-grandfather, wasn't he?"

We walked a ways before he answered, "Yep."

"Did he have a family?"

A long pause before he found his tongue. "Yep."

I could see firing questions at him wouldn't speed the conversation, so I slowed to his pace. After a while, I asked, "How many children?"

He seemed to dredge his answers one word at a time from a channel of confusion. "Two."

We walked in silence for a few minutes.

"What were their names?"

Another dozen steps. "Ezra and Levi."

I sensed he was devoid of emotion and lacked sentimentality. Each answer demanded an effort in itself. Then suddenly, he burst forth with a whole sentence.

"Probably woulda had more 'cept he married late and died young."

As we mounted the front porch steps, I asked, "How'd he die?"

He scratched his head, walked across the porch and pulled a bottle of beer from a cooler. I refused his offer. Half sitting on the rail, his shifting eyes scanned me twice before he found the word, "Crucified." The dullness in his tone suggested crucifixion was an ordinary event that he didn't much care about one way or the other. As for me, I gasped and gulped for air before I could continue.

"Crucified! You mean crucified like on a cross?"

"No." He shrugged. The beer disappeared in three long pulls. "Wasn't like that." He staggered to the cooler. When I refused, he pulled another from the ice and shoved the empty in upside down. I could see plenty of inverted bottles. He returned to his perch on the rail with his back against a post, gazed into space and said nothing. This is the story I pried from him during the next hour.

Elijah was the eldest son of Luke and Rebecca; born in 1831, a restive boy as smart as they come. His parents sent him to boarding school in Pennsylvania. He returned in 1860 educated in arts and

LOST RIVER BRIDGE

religion bringing the philosophy of John Wesley with him. For ten years, the Quakers and the Baptists had argued about the replacement church for the one that burned in 1850. Attendance dwindled at prayer meetings until the residents of Lost River Bridge seemed to abandon religion. In less than a year, Elijah Pursey brought an end to the squabbling and united the community in the name of the First Methodist Church.

I left Lou asleep on the hammock. Homeward bound, I wondered about his devotion to his beloved great-grandfather that he described as one might expect a son to talk about a loving parent.

Several days later I talked with Uncle Henry alone on the patio.
"You know anything about Elijah Pursey?"
"Sure. Everybody knows 'bout him. He's a saint 'round here."
"Really. What did he do to become famous?"

Uncle Henry clambered down the family tree more or less echoing drunken Lou. He sidetracked into religion during the Civil War talking about ignored preachers reminding the armies on both sides the Lord said, "Thou shalt not kill." But the war was about killing and the killers wanted the preacher to say the Lord bet on their side and would overlook the law about killing Damn Yankees or Johnny Rebs. Not many preachers obliged with contrived bigotry and so they watched their flocks drift away on rafts of misdirected patriotism. Elijah became a traveling salesman taking religion to the hills. He finished building his church. When war came in 1861, he left to serve in the battlefields. He returned in 1865.

Meanwhile, the jayhawkers spread fear and destruction; killing, looting and burning throughout Missouri and Kansas. Elijah couldn't do much to persuade people to attend church. He rode through the hills as an emissary of the Lord pleading His cause and casting seeds of love. He didn't carry a firearm believing the Lord protected him. He preached no harm could come to those who honored our Father. Folks swallowed their fear and put their trust in Elijah, if not the Lord. Then a terrible catastrophe happened.

"On a Sunday morning—why, Lizzie's calling us in to eat."

The day came to mow the big cemetery across the road from the church. Emery started at first light between half past five and six. For four hours, we worked like pack mules. In the heat of the day, we talked more than we worked. After the sun settled behind the mountain, we did a few more hours until nightfall. Our cemetery days ran sixteen or seventeen hours, half of them working and half talking.

"Emery," I said as I leaned against a tree trunk gnawing a piece of grass, "I understand Elijah Pursey built the church in 1860. Gee! Almost ninety years ago."

"Yep!"

We sat silently while I searched for the switch to start his talk.

"He was a great man, wasn't he?"

"Yep!"

It seemed dubious that one man built the church alone.

"Your paw said he built it himself."

"Paw never drove a nail in that church. Built 'fore he was born."

Ignition! Feed him a little controversy.

"Your paw didn't build it? He said he did." I hoped my lie never reached Uncle Henry's ears.

"He's lying."

"Who?"

"Paw."

"Why?"

"'Cause Elijah built it by hisself."

"Lou Pursey said jayhawkers crucified his great-grandfather."

"That's a lie."

"Tell me what happened."

"Come here."

We walked across the road to the double-door entry. He ran his hand over the right hand leaf.

"There," he said. "See that." His finger pointed at a small notch. "That's where they pinned him."

"What do you mean, pinned him?"

"Drove a knife through his hand and pinned him to the door."

LOST RIVER BRIDGE

I remembered if I even hinted at disbelief, he'd turn off. I bit my tongue and swallowed hard. He didn't notice my hesitation because he had not finished pointing out the evidence. I watched his finger trace a pattern around a dark spot below the gouge.

"That's Elijah's blood."

I examined an oblong irregular patch that may or may not have been blood. Experts could easily discover the exact nature of the dark patch. I imagined a bloodstain would weather off after ninety years. It might be only an odd curl in the grain. I examined it in detail, but withheld my Doubting Thomas reaction.

"Gee! That's amazing. Tell me what happened."

His voice changed to a tone I never heard him use before. The terse speech shifted to transitory passion. For the first time, his eyes reflected excitement and I knew he loved this story.

"It happened during a Sunday morning service. Most everybody in church heard yelling and cursing through the open windows. Next thing they heard was rifle fire. Nobody ever agreed on how many shots. Some said only one, others claimed they heard at least three. No matter, the women and kids was scared half to death, and rightly so with all that shooting and cursing.

"An ugly, smelly, unshaven jayhawker, wearing a confederate jacket and red bandanna tied around his head, strode down the aisle waving a pistol. With fire in his eyes, he grabbed the front of Elijah's shirt and pulled him up until only his toes touched the floor. He dangled him like a hung turkey, shook him like a hound dog playing with a rag doll and flung him away. Elijah fell backwards, tripped over the step at the altar and crashed to the floor. He lay there unconscious with the whole congregation just a setting like ghosts watching blood trickle from his head.

"'Get out,' the guerrilla yelled.

"When they come out from the church, they saw a jayhawker lying in the middle of the road. He was as dead as dead with his skull busted open.

"'On accounta somebody killed me brother here,' the bully said, 'five of youse is gonna die 'less you tell me who done this.'

"Them jayhawkers pushed five old men against the wall. Their wives and children was watching. Can you imagine! Five men lined up waiting to be shot with their families watching, tears running down their faces and not a single thing they can do 'bout it; and them bandits sneering and aiming their guns.

"'Who done this?' The captain shouted. 'One more minute 'fore your daddies die 'less one of youse tells me who done this.'

"Elijah Pursey come staggering out the door. He fell against the jayhawk leader, near pushed him over. 'I fired the shot,' he said.

"The captain pushed Elijah to the ground with a real dirty laugh. His spit flew from 'tween his teeth and landed on Elijah's bloody head. 'Tie the murdering priest to a tree, boys. I'm going to have a game of William Tell.'

"They set an apple core on Elijah's head. The captain aimed. 'Don't move,' he said. The bullet split the tree. A woman screamed. Elijah slumped. The apple tumbled to the ground.

"'The chicken-liver fainted,' roared the boss. 'What kind of man is this? I tell you, boys, he ain't no man of God. He can't face death. Crucify the devil. Nail him to the church door, boys.'

"They propped Elijah against the door, holding his arms spread-eagle and drove a knife through his left hand. A shot rang out. The jayhawk leader fell. Another shot; another body hit the ground; three dead jayhawkers littered the road. The others fled. Out from the woods stepped Lucien Bellechase and his three sons. 'Course they done that on account of Elijah was married to a Bellechase girl.

"They carried Elijah into the church and dressed his wound. The next Sunday, with hand bandaged up, he blessed the Bellechase family. The folks crowded the church, if not to praise God, then to praise the heroism of Elijah Taber Pursey who didn't seem his usual self. Strange! You know, he never took the bandage from off his hand. He died at the age of thirty-six; and lies buried round back near the door to his church."

I had never seen Emery so moved. I thought he might cry. His voice softened so I could scarcely hear him. "But he never really died. Near every family in Lost River Bridge had an ancestor in church that day. He saved them all. Gave his life. How is it he had the courage to sacrifice himself? What do you think, Elijah?"

I crossed the road pondering Emery's heartfelt performance and sat in the shade of a tree searching for an answer.

"There's no explaining, Emery. I don't know except to say he got his reward in Heaven."

Emery plunked down beside me and lit the cigarette I offered.

"He's in Heaven all right. I know that for sure 'cause he ain't in the cemetery."

"What do you mean? You said he's buried by the church door."

"He is, but he don't live there. He's gone."

"Where?"

"To Heaven like you said."

For a moment, I lacked the courage to ask the obvious. I took a deep breath and hoped I wouldn't offend him.

"You mean some souls still hang around the cemetery?"

He shrugged and picked his teeth. "Yep."

"Who?"

"Granny Sarah's still here. Frieda too, but I don't often see her."

"How do you know?"

"I talk to Granny. Something ain't finished in their lives."

"Like what? Give me a for instance."

"She told me about the Saint Christopher medal."

"What about it?"

"Somebody stole it out of Frieda's coffin."

"Who?"

"Frieda thinks Mark Pursey done it. He come to her funeral. Late that night after they sealed her coffin, she says he stole it."

"Where is it now?"

"Granny thinks Elijah Pursey had it. When she asked him, he pretended he couldn't hear her. At least, that's what she says."

"So where is it now?"

"I don't know. The ants can't find it. I think Lou Pursey knows. That's why he drinks so much."

Episode Seven

Abby Watson

On a quiet evening after supper, I stood on the bridge abutment and threw a few twigs in the river to make sure the water flowing uphill was not a dream. Meandering along to the Emporium, I sat on the porch bench, watched the passing scene and enjoyed my moment of solitude away from endless storytelling. Beliefs that I held to be true came unglued in absurd tales. Water flowed uphill, ghosts talked with the living and ants carried messages from the grave. Worst of all, friends greeted one another with live ammunition. I wondered if any philosophy explained such behavior. Traditional beliefs that I thought everybody more or less accepted seemed pushed aside. Life in Lost River Bridge verged towards insanity or senselessness; or perhaps just plain craziness. These folks existed for hundreds of years in a self-governing, lawless community that considered lying a religious rite. The outside world held little meaning in lives that enshrined the deeds of the dead and the living in dubious legends. I sat on the bench thinking about their nonsense when the door pushed open. A woman stepped out of the Emporium.

"Elijah!" She looked both ways, brushed the bench with a white handkerchief and sat tilting towards me. "I have wanted to talk to you so badly." She drew the word *so* out as if had ten *o*'s. Her head turned to the right, then to the left and her voice dropped to a whisper. "Could you … would you—"

"Sure," I said. "But why don't you start by telling me who you are."

A blush colored her unadorned cheeks. Both hands carried the white handkerchief to her face, covering her mouth and chin as if shielding some secret embarrassment. The hands were big, farmwife hands that had performed more than their share of hard toil. Her face projected beauty beneath a brow lined with worry. I guessed she was forty-five; an attractive picture in her long gingham dress. A wedding band did not surprise me.

"Oh! I'm sorry. My name's Abigail Watson."

"Nice to meet you, Mrs. Watson."

"Please! Call be Abby,"

"Sure, Abby. What can I do for you?"

She rose. Again, the eyes surveyed right and left.

"Not here."

I suspected another story and wanted to say I'd had enough but the stealthy glances suggested something unusual in her anxiety.

"I don't know where we could go," I said. "Let me carry your parcels and you lead the way."

"Well, it's just that—"

"I understand. Lead the way."

We crossed the road toward the log-meeting house, chatting as we went. Was I enjoying my visit? Was this the first time I ever met Henry and Lizzie? Wasn't Emery a funny man? I learned he often walked her daughter home. She led me around the back where several spectator benches ringed a pitch court for playing horseshoes.

"We could ... ." She paused with quick right and left head-shifts "Sit down, Elijah. We could talk here. Would this be all right?"

"It's all right with me."

"Nobody will hear us."

"I guess not."

She ran her hands down her rump and to the sides of her thighs preparing to sit when she suddenly muttered the single word, "Oh!" I stood motionless holding her packages and watching the performance. Out came the white hankie. Holding one corner, she used it as a duster along the bench although I couldn't see anything that called for removal. Again, she performed her ritual in preparation for sitting. This time she sat and spread her skirt demurely and, I thought, rather unnecessarily since it reached almost to her ankles.

"It's about Lou," she said.

"Lou?"

"Lou Pursey. My brother."

She poured out his problems in a monologue of woe that grew steadily worse the longer she spoke. His heavy drinking, she insisted, had reached epidemic proportions. Slovenly in his dress, erratic work habits, irresponsible about his meals and she said, her lips close to my ear and tears swelling in her eyes, "he smells."

"Abby, I'm sorry but what can I do about it?"

"You were in the military. Everybody says you were."

The connection between my military career and her depraved brother escaped me. When I nodded affirmatively trying to gather my wits, she didn't wait for me to speak.

"Then you understand."

"I do?"

She rose and gathered her parcels while I looked on in bewilderment. Without warning, she kissed my cheek.

"Sweet of you. I'll look for you in the morning. What do you like for breakfast?"

"Breakfast?"

"Then afterwards you can help Lou pick the corn. It's ripe now. I'll tell him that's why you came. That'll give you a chance to talk to him alone. See you in the morning." With a cheery smile and a wave of the white handkerchief, she sailed off having accomplished her mission.

Morning came all too soon. Since I enjoy an early walk, I marched the two and a half miles to Abby's home, the same place where I talked with Lou, not recognizing at the time that he was Abby's brother. I arrived a little after seven. Three children, varying in age from about ten to nineteen, answered my knock. They opened the door wide and I saw Abby standing in the passage to the kitchen.

"My! You start early."

"You didn't say what time you served breakfast."

She looked flustered and, I sensed, embarrassed. The children raced to the kitchen and I followed.

"Have a cup of coffee. I'll finish feeding the kids. Then I'll fix something for you."

LOST RIVER BRIDGE

"Did I misunderstand?"

"Oh, heavens no! I just didn't think you'd be here so early. Take your coffee and sit in the parlor. It won't be long."

I entered a small, square room with two unmatched easy chairs, a reading lamp and a pre-war floor-model Philco radio. Haphazard wallpaper covered two sides of the room; the other two displayed dark blue fabric from floor to ceiling fastened with thumbtacks. I peeked behind the drapes to see unpainted plywood veneer reclaimed from old tea crates; mighty cold and drafty in winter. Well-worn paperback editions of romance and mystery novels littered the top of a two-layer bookshelf made from boards supported on concrete bricks. Some children's literature, several coloring books, crayons and various board games cluttered the lower shelves. At the end away from the door, a large, black leather-bound volume stood upright against the brick support. I knew instantly it was the family Bible. We had one in our home in Quebec that looked the same.

"Mind if I look at your family Bible?"

"No. By all means help yourself."

I took the big book from the shelf and settled into the chair by the light. The first few pages recorded family births, marriages and deaths. The entries started with the marriage of Luke and Rebecca, records of their children with several dates followed by question marks. I skipped through the family history to the birth of Elijah Taber Pursey. The records of his life, marriage and children, written in a careful hand, were easy to read; the same hand that made all the other entries to this point. The next entry recorded the date of Elijah's death written in a different hand that I guessed was that of a female. The next entry referenced a letter from California reporting Ezra's death. In yet another hand, I read *pasted letter in back* with no date. The Pursey family record ended.

On the second to last page, I detected a couple of stains that could have been paste marks but I found no sign of the letter. I flipped to the back cover. Unable to detect any marks, I ran my fingers lightly over the page. Nothing! A soft cardboard paper lined the inside back cover. Again, I ran my fingers down the page like a blind man reading Braille. I don't know why I did it. I didn't expect to discover anything but suddenly I stopped. Halfway down the page, I felt a roughness in the texture. Tilting the book back and forth in the light, I could not distinguish anything yet I could feel it. Something had embossed the paper. I sat back and folded my arms, wondering. The children's coloring books caught my eye. Thumbing through them, I found a tracing book. I placed a sheet of the thin paper over the embossed cardboard and gently rubbed with a lead pencil. The top of a circle appeared; too big for a silver dollar. I guessed a souvenir. Ulysses Grant, I bet. I remembered a medallion I bought at the World's Fair in New York in 1939. A head appeared, then a hand holding a staff. Our whole class went on charter buses. Four days in New York and most of us too young to appreciate it. Funny looking nose; whoever had a nose like that? Maybe they call it aquiline. Mustache covering the mouth. Beard dangling down from the chin. We threw pillows out the hotel window. I suppose the chaperone scolded us; I don't remember. Letters! Looks like an *S* on the left; an *R* on the right. I felt my breath coming faster. Good Lord! *ST* on the left and a dot followed by a *C*; looks like part of an *H* followed by *ER* on the right. It couldn't be! My hand trembled. I had to stop, get control lest I tear the paper. Emery! Emery, you won't believe this. It can't be. It's impossible. Finish it. Go on! At last, the completed picture revealed St. Christoper. It really was! But it couldn't possibly be the same one. Could it be? I tore the tracing from the book, folded it carefully and put it in my shirt pocket. I felt around the perimeter for an opening, the insertion point. Nothing! I felt the binding along the spine. I found a slight distortion, possibly three inches, long enough for a flat blade to sweep under the cardboard lining and recover the object. The cut in the page, expertly slit and carefully sealed, was unnoticeable except under close examination. I had no idea how the medallion got there but I knew how the culprit removed it. I closed the book, returned it to its place and started for the kitchen to tell Abby thanks for the invitation but I had to leave.

"What you doing here?"

I swung around.

"Oh! Good morning, Lou. Your sister asked me over to help pick corn."

LOST RIVER BRIDGE

He leaned against the kitchen wall not two feet from me looking terrible, worse than a skid row bum; an unshaven derelict exuding an unpleasant odor. I felt sorry for Abby and her kids.

"Ain't picking today," Lou grumbled.

Abby hurried from the kitchen wiping her hands on her apron.

"Of course we are." She smiled in a way so patently forced it made me wince.

He spoke to her in a vicious tone. Voices grew loud. Lou's language turned blue. Abby shooed the children away with a hand wave. He clenched his teeth and latched on to her upper arm with his right hand. I stepped towards them and grabbed Lou's wrist

"Let go, Lou."

"Get out of here and mind your own business."

"I'm getting out, Lou, because it's not my business to interfere in a family quarrel. But your sister asked me to help her and that's what I'm going to do. Don't you hurt her because I'm coming back and if I find you so much as touched a hair on her head, I'm going to thrash you to within an inch of your life."

His eyes flashed defiance that I thought camouflaged an inner fear. It was more than fear. It was terror. I had seen it in Germany when I lost my bearings on a late night patrol. One of the boys turned pale and began to weep. He was inconsolable even after our safe return. In the second that I met Lou's eyes, I knew he harbored a terrifying phantom in his soul that he could not conquer. He lunged toward me but his emaciated deplorable state precluded a fight. His blow was weak. I pushed back and he tumbled into a chair. Abby hissed like a cat and returned to the kitchen. I left them to fight it out for better or for worse.

At nine thirty, I reached Uncle Henry's house. He was in the barn doing his chores. Lizzie performed the Tuesday ritual at the ironing board. Eager to show Emery my prize, I hurried to the church and burst through the door. He looked like a statue sitting on the altar step with his arms folded across his chest, his eyes staring blankly into space, deep in a trance. I came to an abrupt halt and wondered to whom he talked this time. He shook his head like a dog coming out of water. His eyes blinked a couple of times. Then he smiled and asked a question that stunned me.

"Where did you find it?"

Emery listened to my story as if he had heard it before. It bored him; his ennui annoyed me.

"I knew Lou had it," he said.

"Lou doesn't have it. It wasn't there."

"If he doesn't have it, he knows where it is."

"Come on, Emery. We don't even know if it's Granny Sarah's medallion."

"It's hers all right."

"How do you know?"

"She told me."

I gave up. No amount of talk would ever persuade me his extra sensory perception was in tune with the dead. My exasperation obscured my mission so I changed the subject.

"Tell me about Abby Watson."

"Oldest Pursey girl. Great-granddaughter of Elijah. Married Timothy Watson. Killed in the desert; 1942, I think. Patton's Army."

"She gets a pension, I suppose. What else does she do to earn a living?"

"Sells vegetables in the summer. Cleaning and washing for Gainesville folks in the winter."

A sense of guilt enveloped me; a gnawing distress rumbled in my innards and radiated to my brain.

"Come on, Emery. Let's go."

"Where?"

"To pick corn."

Episode Eight

Abner's Dogs

The longer I remained in Lost River Bridge, the more I understood the ties binding the community. Families in the Eastern Townships of Quebec shared no comparable sense of unity. My grandparents encouraged my father and mother to attend university, leave home and improve their lot. I gained the impression mountain people discourage their offspring from moving out of their home. If the children go for educational reasons, parents expect them to return as Elijah Pursey did. Failure to return to the mountain home breaks a branch off the family tree. A letter arrives—if anybody cares to take the time to write it—announcing a death. The event goes unrecorded in the family Bible. The letter, inexpertly glued in the back, disappears, the branch severed and gone. Either you are in the family or you are out. The ins tell their legends to one another for hundreds of years. The outs are forgotten, deleted from the family heritage, erased unceremoniously from the stories. The stay-at-homes and the wanderers never communicate, existing in two different worlds with unequal values and no common denominator except the surname. After the experience at Abby's house, I imagined I might be a bridge in some mysterious way between two different offshoots. Perhaps I could mend a branch of the broken tree, but not on this Sunday.

Abner Applehorn treated Sunday as a family day; church in the morning and participation in community affairs in the afternoon, and finally, the traditional storytelling in the evening. I guessed he passed it on because Henry and Lizzie often followed the same ritual. In modern times, radio supplanted storytelling, rocking chairs and corn-cob pipes. When guests arrived, custom took over with the radio turned off as if it never existed. I was to remember this night a few weeks later. I had never seen such a glow in Emery's eyes. Lizzie explained his dreamy look, whispering in my ear.

I think he's got a girl," she said.

Harvey Hooper, his wife, Angela, and Harvey's ninety-six-year-old father came for supper. Eleven of us rocked and smoked on the patio behind the house when Lizzie said, "Henry, tell the story about daddy's dog." He needed no encouragement.

With reverential pride, Henry burst into a long speech about Grandpa's farm in the Bryant River valley. He talked about planting and harvesting, milking and tending the herd, roping and calving. The nostalgia almost brought tears to his eyes as he recalled mules pulling the plows, men reaping with hand-held scythes and farm horses dragging hay carts through the valley to the barn.

With Harvey's help, Mr. Hooper managed to get his pipe lit after half a dozen tries. With the smoke billowing around his head, he barged into the story. I could hardly understand the old man who croaked like a frog, holding his pipe between his teeth as he talked.

"I 'member thet barn. Gone now, ain't it, Son?"

"Yes, Dad."

"What happened to it? Burned down, Son?"

"No, Dad. Why don't you listen to Henry? He's telling the story."

"Thet's what I'm doing, Son. Got a match?"

I felt a little uncomfortable, but everybody paused while Harvey helped his father fire the pipe. Maybe seniority mattered; if the old man wanted to tell the story, I think local tradition deferred to the eldest person present. In a moment, he continued.

Most bootiful barn ever was. More 'n fifty feet high with a square doodad on the roof. What d'cha call them things, Son?"

"Cupola, Dad."

"Yeah. Thet's right; a coopooloo up there on top with a spire what reached near to the sky. On top of thet there coopooloo, Abner stuck a solid gold weathervane so high in the sky ain't no rooster could get up thet high. Thet's why Abner always had grumpy roosters. Henry, tell these young'uns 'bout thet there barn while I light my pipe. Got a match, Son?"

LOST RIVER BRIDGE

Uncle Henry laughed, clapped his hands and continued.

"Like Mr. Hooper said, the barn was a beautiful building, curved wood lintels over the windows and vents in the cupola, equal to anything you ever seen in a European castle. Many a traveler passing by couldn't believe his own eyes; a painted barn in the middle of the prairies. 'Why that just ain't possible,' they'd say, but there it was staring them in the face. Abner picked a gray color for the siding and white for the doors and windows with maroon trim. The rain beating on the metal roof sounded like a Civil War battle."

Drinking coffee on the patio and listening to this description seventy-five years later, I wondered how beautiful Abner's barn would become in another seventy-five years. I interrupted to ask if anyone had pictures of the barn.

"No there aren't any," Lizzie said. "When Daddy died, we searched everywhere. We couldn't find a single picture."

"I'm not surprised," I said. "Go on with the story, Uncle Henry."

"The coyotes and bears roaming the mountains was a threat to the herd. Abner bought trained cattle dogs from the East Coast. Cost a wagonload of money. Problem was them dogs had no sense of how to protect themselves from the wild critters. One by one, coyotes killed off Abner's investment in thoroughbred hounds. He set about to finding a wolfhound that weren't afeared of coyotes and bears, but wouldn't hurt the herd none. On a farm near St. Louis, he found an old mongrel so mean and ornery, the owner wanted to shoot him. When Abner offered two dollars, the fellow grabbed it and said, 'You'll be sorry, Mister.'

"Abner never regretted buying that hound. It had an instinct for cattle. One cowhand, riding 'long side with the dog running loose, could drive the herd in half the time it took them thoroughbreds. Wasn't long afore Abner let the beast loose at night and I tell you what, them critters kept their distance. Abner gave orders to chain the dog in the corral in the daytime. He didn't worry none with the barn and corral way in the valley, but just the same he warned everybody to keep away, especially children."

I wasn't sure how the subject changed so quickly, but suddenly they were praising Abner Applehorn. What a gentle giant; the kindest man ever lived in Lost River Bridge; a softhearted he-man who cared about the birds and the bees. He kept birdseed and lard in the barn to fill the birdfeeders every day. He had a good notion about his supplies. One day he realized the birdseed was disappearing faster than the birds could eat it.

Now, I cain't rightly recall the sheriff's name," Henry said, "but he come out to the barn to look into the stealing what was going on. When he was done, he couldn't pin the theft on a single soul. They tried rattraps and weasel snares, but the stealing didn't stop. Abner figured if he set a dish of seed out in the corral, he could watch to see what come to eat it. He picked a moonlit night so as he could see movement in the corral. He waited as quiet as could be to find out who was stealing his seed. Round about midnight, he heared scratching at the corral gate. Then the gate swung open. Abner stretched his head out from behind the door. He seen the critter all right, but he couldn't make out what it was except it was big. He squeezed out a little farther and gasped. His own hound dog paid no never mind with his head buried in the birdseed dish.

"Abner thought that was the funniest sight he'd ever seen. From then on, the hands set out a dish of birdseed for the dog every night."

"Well," I said, "that's a pretty good tale, Uncle Henry."

He looked at me kind of funny and I realized the story wasn't over. After glancing around to the guests as if to apologize for this Eastern boy's lack of manners, he continued.

"One Sunday morning a few weeks later, Abner went to the barn like he usually done everyday to supervise the milking. The hound had escaped and nobody knew where it had gone. 'Now listen here,' he said, 'you two men get on your horses and warn everybody to be on the lookout. And you don't come back if you ain't found that dog.'

"Abner waited. The men didn't return. He paced back and forth like a father waiting for his wife to have a baby. Still the men didn't come back. It was near time for church. Abner had no choice but to head on home to get ready for the service. He cleaned up and put on his Sunday-go-to-Meeting clothes. He and Effy arrived a few minutes late. The service had begun so they took a pew in the back and opened the hymn books. As Abner looked to see the hymn number,

LOST RIVER BRIDGE

Effy let out a shriek. She stretched out her arm, and pointed her finger. Abner looked. There was the dog, robe and all, singing with the choir."

Thus inspired, Emery contributed a tale about his father.

"Before Grandpa Abner brought the herders from the East Coast, he owned a mongrel the color of maple syrup poured over pancakes. He stood as tall as a German shepherd, ran as graceful as a greyhound, herded cattle like a border collie, and hunted like a retriever.

"Now, Grandpa had a twenty-five-year-old mule, leastwise that's how old he said it was. The second day Henry worked on the farm, Grandpa told him to harness the mule and plow the garden.

"Papa went on out to the barn holding the bridle for to drop it over the mule's ears, but the mule backed off. He tried once more. Again, the mule backed off. Finally, the mule was in the corner and couldn't back no more, but it still hadn't put his head up for Henry to slip the bridle on. Suddenly, the mule kicked at the ground, raised his head and said, 'I ain't working today; it's too hot.'

"Henry didn't know what to do on accounta he ain't never heard a mule talk. Then he come to realize Abner played a joke on him. He started back to the house just as Abner came out followed by the dog. Henry asked Abner how he done that.

"'Done what?' Abner asked.

"'Got the mule to talk,' says Henry.

"Well, they got into an argument, Abner thinking Henry was making up stories, and Henry thinking Abner played a joke. Finally, they agreed to try again. Henry took the bridle just as he did the first time. The mule backed until it was cornered by the fence. Suddenly, it raised his head and said, 'Told you I ain't working today, it's too hot.'

"Grandpa leaned against the fence, eyes as big as saucers. His mouth opened and closed, but no sound came out. Finally, he managed to speak.

"'My gosh,' he said, 'I never heard a mule talk afore.'

"'Me neither,' said the dog.

Episode Nine

Herman and Gerda

Walking by and not noticing whatever it is you are supposed to notice always upsets people. I came down to breakfast to find Aunt Lizzie cleaning the stove. She didn't raise her head, and she didn't answer when I said good morning. I guessed I didn't react to something or other. If somebody asked, I would have probably said she'd been in the kitchen since daybreak. That wasn't true. She'd been picking vegetables. They were on the counter near the sink; fresh-cut flowers, too, on the windowsill in a blue vase. Lizzie asked what I wanted for breakfast. Right away, I knew something was wrong because she never asked what I wanted to eat unless she was upset. Uncle Henry walked in, sat down, and didn't see the vegetables or the flowers either. No use saying sorry because she'll say if you're sorry you'd do something about it. So I strolled over to the window casual like.

"Where's Emery this morning? My, aren't those beautiful flowers! Look at these flowers, Uncle Henry."

I couldn't fool Lizzie, but I could pacify her because she was dying to talk, and it was going to be about Emery. She doted on Emery, not to the exclusion of the other kids, but she talked about him by name. She referred to the others as *boys, girls*—both singular and plural—*you there* and *the lot of you* depending on which particular chore she assigned to whom. Emery had the knack of heroism in his mother's eyes. Most of the time he could do no wrong. He was house trained, domesticated, you might say. The others resisted obedience school with various forms of rebellion.

LOST RIVER BRIDGE

"Emery grew those flowers." She turned to look at me, her back to the cold stove, a swagger in her voice. "Vegetables too," she added. As she crossed the room the swagger became visible. She opened the door to the porch, holding it for me to step outside. She took my arm, and led me down the steps beaming like a bride walking down the aisle, her right arm looped through my left.

"We'll have flowers all summer long. Emery grows them by hisself 'cept when I send the boys and girls to weed. Look here at the vegetables. It's early August, and look at the size of those pumpkins."

"Gee, Aunt Lizzie, the garden impressed me from the first day I was here."

Her left hand covered her open mouth as she gasped. I thought she was going to choke, but the hand fell away She turned slightly; her eyes met mine. She looked pretty, which is an unusual way to describe Aunt Lizzie with her misaligned teeth and slightly crooked Applehorn mouth.

"The Lord will punish you for lying, Elijah. Ain't it a beautiful garden? You never took no time to look at it careful like, did you, Elijah?"

She walked me around the garden. When we went back in, she didn't ask what I'd like for breakfast.

Emery was on his knees behind the church when I arrived. He didn't notice me while I scanned the property, and the new cemetery across the road. The grounds were immaculate, the flowers beautiful, the hedges and bushes trimmed where they should be trimmed, and not trimmed were they shouldn't be. Aunt Lizzie had opened my eyes to his remarkable talent. The impact of his devotion to his work invoked a sense of guilt, or was it shame? He had been tending the church property alone since the age of fifteen. I classified him as a kooky storyteller without recognizing his real talent; I had never uttered a word of acclaim for his fine work.

"Hello, Emery! How's it going?"

"Hot."

"I've brought a thermos of iced tea. Come on. Take a break."

STEPHEN P. BYERS

We sat in the shade near the grave of Elijah Pursey. I poured the tea, flipped him a cigarette, and wondered how to break the conversational ice. He laid his right hand, palm down, on the grass. In a few moments, an ant scurried along his index finger and stopped on the back of his hand. I made no pretense of hiding my interest, and leaned over for a clear view. He raised his left arm to prevent me from coming too close, but I could see the little creature. I will swear on a stack of Bibles that black body stood on its hind legs with its head tilted up. Suddenly, it hurried off. I thought of the white rabbit and wondered if ants carried pocket watches. We finished our smoke. I poured a second cup of tea. For at least fifteen minutes, we did not speak, although I confess, I found it difficult to keep my mouth shut. At last, he spoke.

"The ant said Elijah Pursey is hanging around."

I bit my lip to keep from laughing.

"Got a problem, has he?"

"Don't know."

He signaled the end of the conversation by handing me the cap to the thermos and getting to his feet. I followed him to the back fence. He didn't ask if I intended to work; he simply held out his shears and told me to trim along the fence line.

At lunch, I took advantage of his silence to initiate a conversation about the grounds. I couldn't see any point in lying so I told him exactly the way I felt.

"Emery, I owe you an apology. I've been here with you a good many times this summer but until today I didn't realize what a swell job you've done."

He blushed and waggled his head back and forth. I knew he appreciated my compliments. In his usual reticent manner, several minutes passed before he felt comfortable enough to talk. Then, like an oil well erupting, the talk gushed forth. He explained how he pleaded with the elders in 1939 for permission to look after the grounds. Of course, they said he was too young, but he got the job because his mother went to bat for him. One by one, he built new planting beds. Then he shifted his attention to the lawns. Next came bushes and shrubs. Then came his plans. He wanted to install wrought iron fencing across the front; remove the wood entrance steps replacing them in stone with a canopy over the doors; build a concrete curb and drain the parking lot properly. More than anything else, he wanted a steeple and a church bell.

"But the church don't have the money to pay for that stuff. I put a box inside the front door marked Church Improvements. Every week I collect a few dollars and you mark my words, Elijah, afore I die I'll get every one of my jobs done."

As if to follow Aunt Lizzie's canon—if you're truly sorry, do something about it—I committed myself to work with Emery every day. The only exception was a few hours off because I wanted to find out if Abby was having trouble with her drunken brother. Her gratitude overflowed when I visited because all the corn had sold in one weekend. She and Irene never sold the entire crop so fast, not that anything I did made it happen.

"That's wonderful, Abby, but I came to ask about Lou."

She put her head down, and turned away. Despite my coaxing, she wouldn't talk about her brother. There was no sign of him in the fields or the house, and I concluded he was off somewhere getting drunk.

"Abby," I said as I was about to leave after tea, "there is only one thing I want to know. Did Lou hurt you?"

"No," she said. "I'm grateful to you and Emery for picking the corn, but you shouldn't have threatened him." I looked puzzled, I guess, because she didn't hesitate to remind me what I'd said. "You told him, if he hurt me you'd thrash him within an inch of his life." She began crying. Silent tears tumbled down her cheeks. She held a white handkerchief to her eyes. I waited for her to recover. In a moment she caught her breath, and continued. "I know you meant well ... ." Her tears came again. When I tried to comfort her, she pushed me away. Suddenly, she blurted out her trouble. "He left home after you spoke to him, and he ain't come back since." She turned and fled.

"Emery," I said after supper as we sat in the patio, "I feel really bad about Lou and Abby. Maybe I'm responsible for him leaving."

"Heard what you said to him."

I suppose a remark like that should have surprised me, but with Emery nothing he said, no matter how perceptive, surprised me. Instead, it raised my curiosity.

"Where'd you hear?"

"I hear a lot."

He averted his eyes, and behaved like a grade school kid reciting an *I-know-something-you-don't-know* singsong. A smirk and superior look destroyed the image of mature responsibility.

"Who from? The ants or Granny Sarah?"

The moment I spoke, I regretted those words. My object was to cultivate him, not alienate him. Strangely enough, he wasn't offended.

"Neither," he said.

I stubbed out my cigarette.

"Time to go to work. What do you want me to do today?"

He looked a little crestfallen. An ant ran along his arm. His eyes followed it. He nodded his head from side to side. The ant left. I waited in silence. I didn't dare break the spell by looking at my watch. It seemed like an hour passed but it probably was no more than ten minutes. As happened so often, when he finally spoke, he flabbergasted me.

"Grandpa Abner was mighty upset paying a hundred twenty-five dollars for Lizzie. Leastwise, he made like he was upset but the truth is he was awful happy Effy come home alive. I don't know 'bout where you come from, but round here women died all the time bringing children into the world. Without Granny Effy to tend to him and his kids, Abner woulda had a tough row to hoe. He couldn't forget that there ride to Mountain Home in the carriage. Today it ain't much—two, three hours maybe—but in them days it was a long way; took two or three days. And Granny moaning and groaning in the back. Had to put up somewhere at night. And get food and all that stuff. Good thing she wasn't in labor. Makes you wonder if it wasn't pretty dumb to take her all that way. But then, what works out right, I guess, ain't dumb. Everything did work out

LOST RIVER BRIDGE

too, except for Grandpa Abner being so upset.

"He kept telling folks he was going to do something 'bout it. Lost River Bridge needed a doctor and he'd make it his job to find one. Few years later, he got Doc Schumacher to come live here. Nobody's real sure how he done that. It was round 1915. Mama was eleven years old and she says she 'members when her daddy came back with Doc and his wife. Abner took the train north to a place called Berlin in Canada somewheres. Lots of Germans lived there and the war was on and maybe the Canadians didn't like all them blockheads in the middle of their country."

"I think they're called square heads, Emery." He stopped talking and I feared I'd turned him off. His hand roamed through the grass like he was looking for an ant to talk to. Competing with an insect for his attention could have been a humiliating experience had I let it, but no ant arrived. After a lengthy pause, he continued

"Most folks believe Doc come to a little place like this to hide. Everybody was afraid of him ... . Naw! That ain't right. Everybody was afraid of Gerda, his wife. Grandpa built a house for them. It's way down the road and half way up the mountain. You seen it?"

I shook my head but I wasn't interrupting again even with the simple word no.

"It's ell-shaped with a place for them to live at one end, and four rooms that are sort of like a hospital at the other. Folks can rest up there from whatever they have, or women can have their young ones. But it isn't Doc what makes it work; it's Gerda. You never seen such a mismatched pair; little skinny old Doc and big Gerda strong enough to twirl him round her little finger. She scrubs the floor everyday until there ain't no pattern on the linoleum. Then she washes the walls, and when she's done she complains how dirty everything is, and she scrubs the whole place again the next day.

"After they come here and was in the house, Doc set to and fixed scratched knees and broken arms. Pretty soon folks begun to like him and nowadays everybody goes to him with their troubles."

A scowl crossed his brow as if a brand new idea entered his mind.

"When you think about it, 'course they do. Don't have no other choice 'cept to ride to Gainesville where the Doc ain't one bit better. But if somebody's really sick, Gerda don't let Doc do nothing. She tells them to go to Gainesville, or West Plains, or some other place on accounta Doc can't handle it in their little place. Everybody trusts her. Funny how they work; Doc shows up at the sick bed, takes a temperature maybe, feels the pulse, then he leaves, sometimes without saying much of anything. In a little while he's back. It's like he always has to ask Gerda.

"There's other stuff too. If folks don't have no money to pay the bill, then Gerda accepts food instead. Folks pay for treatment with squirrels, or deer, or pumpkin pies. And it was Grandpa Abner made it happen and that's why folks are always telling you he's the savior of Lost River Bridge."

"Neat story," I said. "Lost River Bridge is sure lucky to have a doctor. Wonder why he'd stay in a place like this? I mean, when he could go to a big city hospital and make more money."

Emery shifted his position and his eyes glared at me, his voice filled with frustration.

"It ain't over yet."

"Sorry, Emery. I was only thinking what a great savior your grandfather was."

"I told you, it ain't over yet."

I nodded and kept quiet, fearing I might be replaced by an ant and never hear the end of the tale. I was prepared for almost anything except what came next.

"Lou Pursey broke the Commandments. You know the Good Book says 'honor your father and your mother.' Lou didn't do that. His father was a nice enough man, I guess. Well, maybe pretty tough, really. He only had the two kids and them fifteen years apart. Mr. Pursey loved Abby. Maybe he didn't want more than one child. Anyway, Lou fought with his father all the time. He ran away from home a few times. Didn't go far 'cause they'd catch him and bring him back. Somewhere around age ten, Lou begun to have trouble talking; started stuttering and couldn't seem to remember nothing. The next winter Lou got sick. I mean, real sick, like most everybody thought he'd die. His mama took him to Doc and Gerda.

LOST RIVER BRIDGE

He was there near a month. Folks say Gerda told his daddy and mama, Lou should go to the city hospital, but Mr. Pursey wouldn't allow that. He said to keep him, or put him out in the barnyard with the hens if they liked, but Lou wasn't going to no hospital, and Mr. Pursey wasn't paying for it if he did. That's when Abby stepped into the fight. She loved her brother; always has. The next year—Lou was twelve and Abby was already married—she helped him run away from home. But he didn't run far. He ran to Doc and Gerda, and they hid him in their part of the house like he was their son. Everybody says Mr. Pursey knew where his son was, but he didn't want him at home so he pretended he didn't know. Lou lived at Doc's for near five years. It was good for him, and he was just a normal kid."

"Emery," I said, "I know the story isn't over but I have to ask a question. May I ask my question, please?"

"Well, all right. What is it?"

"You blame Lou for all this. Sounds more like his father caused the trouble."

The Taber chin projected out; a callused left hand caressed it. He scratched his head and looked a little sheepish.

"I guess I left something out."

"What?"

"Lou took a gun to his father."

"He what?"

"He shot his father."

"And hit him?"

"Yep. Hit him."

This struck me like a double whammy. First, the revelation of the boy taking a gun to his father confirmed mental imbalance or unbearable pressure. Second, the confession that Emery, the master storyteller, omitted a key fact was even more startling. I was too stunned to comment.

"Go on with the story," I said.

"Lou left Doc and Gerda to join the navy. During the war, there wasn't no word came back from him. Then, in February 1945, he come home. He'd had … I don't know what you call it … a mental crack up. He come back a basket case mumbling about all kinds of crazy stuff; how cold the water was; and he was going to die in the water; and he couldn't find his life jacket; and he couldn't jump; and the ship was sinking; and he saw a torpedo; and I don't know what else. One time I asked who saved him. He said his great-grandfather, Elijah. When he got drunk, all these problems went away, so he spends his benefits on cheap booze, and he stays half drunk so he can't remember the war. Anyway, Doc and Gerda took him in again. They told him he had to go to one of them head doctors. He wouldn't go. I guess they told Abby they couldn't do nothing and she took him in. And 'cause he's drunk all the time, he can't remember nothing 'bout Granny Sarah's medallion."

"Whoa," I said, not caring if I stopped the story or not. "Wait a minute, Emery! What are you talking about?"

"I told you before Lou Pursey knows the story of the medallion and where it is, but he won't tell me."

It was my turn to ponder. Twenty-four-foot snakes and gowrows tested my beliefs, but this story beat them all. I knew about mentally stressed soldiers breaking down. I didn't believe the US Navy turned their back on battle fatigue without medical treatment.

"Come on, Emery! You're kidding me. Why would the US military turn him loose if he's wacko?"

He looked at me with a triumphant leer.

"See what I mean?"

"No! I don't see what you mean at all."

He shook his head as if I was the dumbest person he'd ever met. A long sigh escaped his grimace.

"For heaven's sakes, Elijah! Of course, they wouldn't turn him loose. The US military hands out benefits for everything. If a serviceman has a sliver because of the war, they look after him for life. But they ain't looking after Lou. Why not?" By this time, Emery was shouting. "I'll tell you why not. Because there ain't one thing wrong with him. He's faking."

I pulled myself to my feet and shrugged.

"I think I'll do a little work pulling weeds," I said.

Episode Ten

Farewell

So it was, at my Mother's suggestion, I spent two months in Missouri. The horror of war was less vivid, the nightmares less violent, and my nerves less edgy. I sent her cards during the summer, and called her often.

"Be starting home soon, Mother. Be there by Labor Day."

At the cemetery, Emery and I cut grass less often, and talked more. Everything slowed. Even the weeds lost interest in propagation. The days were less hot, and the asters would soon bloom. We built new pansy beds, raised above the ground with four-by-six timber borders.

"When do the leaves turn?"

"Late September and on to the end of October."

"Are they bright?"

"Naw! Just a nuisance."

"Why?"

"'Cause I have to rake them. Soon as I do, the wind blows them back."

Storytelling reached a low ebb as if no untold stories remained in Lost River Bridge. We frittered away our time as the number of days before my departure dwindled.

"I think I'll leave Sunday after church."

"How you traveling?"

"Decided to drive."

"What'll you do with the car when you get home?"

"Sell it in Vermont. Customs won't let me take it into Canada."

As always, long pauses interrupted our conversations. We sat with our backs against a tree, drank coffee, and smoked too much. I felt comfortable in this lackadaisical world. I folded my jacket to make a pillow, laid out flat, and closed my eyes. Ten minutes later, he jarred me awake with a surprising question.

"What are you going to talk about Saturday night?"

"Me? Talk? Where?"

"At the party."

"What party?"

"Your going-away party."

I sat bolt upright. He wasn't kidding. Good Lord! They had indoctrinated me, and this was graduation.

Uncle Henry said a few words of introduction after the potluck supper in the old meeting hall. I asked him not to mention army and war. I said I was trying to forget that part of my life. He obliged by calling me a college boy.

"Going back to school. Elijah's going to be an engineer. Soon as he graduates he's coming back here, and he's going to figure out how come our river flows in two directions ... and one of them uphill."

There were thirty-five or forty people in the hall when I rose to speak. I thought I'd be nervous, but I wasn't. My mind flashed back to my mother's kitchen last February twenty-second when I couldn't raise a cup of coffee to my lips without holding it in two hands. I wondered if these folks assembled before me would ever understand how grateful I was for what they'd done for me. Suddenly, I decided the speech I'd thought about was sentimental tripe. I told them a story about gratitude.

"At the start of the summer when I arrived here, I thought how different my home was from yours. I imagined that I might be an agent that could expose the differences so tonight it is my pleasure to tell you there are no differences. You see, you have the illusion that you are on American soil. I hate to be the first to tell you, but that's not true.

"One of your great American heroes is Paul Bunyon. You are all aware he built the Rocky Mountains, and you know he dug the

LOST RIVER BRIDGE

Great Lakes. He cleaned up the debris, and spread it at the foot of the mountains. From the foothills to the Atlantic Ocean, the continent was a flat plain where Paul and his friends played golf.

"A Canadian named Charlie Castor trapped beavers in the lakes of Ontario and Quebec. He was as big as Paul Bunyon, and like Paul, whose partner was Babe the blue ox, he had a partner; a moose called Orignal he trained as a beast of burden.

"Charlie didn't use traps to catch beavers. He waded into the lakes, and slapped his big hand on the water. When the beavers rose to see who called, Charlie plucked them out of the water by the scruff of the neck, and put them in his creel. The beavers were plentiful, and Charlie had difficulty finding places to store them. He built beaver corrals around a few large lakes in northern Ontario, but there were so many beavers the lakes overflowed, and the animals escaped. Then he had to catch them again, which was not only a waste of time, but was also bad for business, and a nuisance to boot.

"One day an old Indian told Charlie about Paul Bunyon digging the Great Lakes. Charlie allowed as how that was a fine idea. He surveyed Canada from coast to coast searching for a piece of flat ground with not too many trees, and not too many rocks, where he could make his own lake. He picked a spot smack dab in the middle of the country, half way between the Atlantic and Pacific Oceans.

"Charlie and Orignal dug deeper and deeper, wider and wider, going farther and farther north, until lifting the dirt out of the hole became a big problem. They solved it by making a long sloping ramp at the south end where they could drag the excavated material out of the hole. The mound to the south became a mountain, and the mountain grew huge. They paid no never mind because Charlie wanted a place for his beavers, and didn't care one hoot about mountains surrounding his lake. In fact, Charlie thought the growing mountains created a scenic view. With a few hotels, he could have his own mountain retreat.

"On they went, farther and farther north. The news of this huge project drifted south. The word reached Paul Bunyon who came to visit. He admired the size of the hole, and admitted it was bigger than anything he'd ever done or heard about anywhere in the world. The respect of such a famous man spurred Charlie to even greater efforts. As winter arrived, the night temperatures fell to thirty or forty below. On the first of December, Charlie surveyed the hole and said to Orignal it was big enough.

"'Yes, sir,' he said, 'just a couple more scoops and then we'll flood her.'

"At sunset with the temperature dropping rapidly, they bust down the end wall. The ocean came roaring in from the north. Charlie and Orignal ran for their lives as a huge tidal wave hundreds of feet high came barreling south. The temperature fell to an all-time low that night. In the morning, Charlie and Orignal couldn't believe their eyes. The water had frozen solid. A huge glacier covered the land as far as they could see.

"Through that cold and miserable winter, the ocean water kept pouring in from the north, freezing and pushing the glacier farther south carrying the mountain of excavated material across the Dakotas, through Nebraska and Iowa, and into Missouri, which was as flat as a pancake at that time. Towards the end of March, the temperature rose, and the ice began to melt. After the cold winter, a warm sunshine greeted the folks in Missouri and Oklahoma. As they prepared to face the spring, a storm brought torrential rains. After the storm, the temperature soared into the nineties. In no time, the ice was gone. There stood the Ozark Mountains, personally delivered by Charlie Castor all the way from Canada with a little help from Mother Nature.

"You folks and your ancestors have lived in the Ozarks for hundreds of years. In all that time, you have never expressed your gratitude to Charlie for providing these mountains that you call home. Since you don't appreciate what Charlie did for you, I want you to know there's a movement in Canada demanding that you give us back our mountains. We intend to put the Ozark Mountains in Saskatchewan, build hotels and create a tourist attraction called the Charlie Castor Memorial Mountain Retreat.

"For those of you who think this tale may not be true, I suggest you look at your high school atlas books. In the middle of Canada, you'll see a big body of water that once upon a time they called Charlie Castor Lake; now they call it Hudson's Bay. At the south end, you'll see James Bay; that's the ramp where Charlie and Orignal dragged out the dirt."

Emery stepped forward and shook my hand.
"I think you qualify as an Ozark storyteller," he said.
I thanked him, shook hands with Uncle Henry, and sat down wondering what came next. Emery signaled to Irene, Abby Watson's oldest daughter, who walked forward and stood beside him.
"Now," Emery said, "I want to make an announcement. It's not a story. It's a fact. Irene and I are going to be married."
He continued to talk for a sentence or two, but the cheers drowned out whatever he said. As I watched the crowd milling about, hugging, kissing, and shaking hands, I realized what a popular figure Emery was. I suppose I was aware of his renown, but it had not really registered. I stood to one side wondering what I could say as I watched the celebration. Then an idea flashed in my mind. I waited until the enthusiasm died a little, then I stepped to the front, and asked for their attention. Emery and Irene stood beside me.
"There's not much I can say to you two except to wish you every happiness. Before I go, I would like to give you a wedding gift. It's a token of my love. Here, Emery and Irene, it's yours."
I handed them the keys to my 1936 Studebaker.

Not long after my return home, I received a gift in the mail from the Canadian Army. As if to apologize for making me their property for the previous three years, they sent me a little cardboard box. In it, I found three medals they awarded to each of several hundred thousand volunteers who served in the European Theater, including me. The Cracker Jack people created the idea; the military went further by not only giving prizes, but also pretending they conferred a measure of prestige. As for bravery, I consider crossing the threshold of the mobilization center my only act of courage. Three years of military service carried me to the edge of moral privation that the kind and gentlepeople of Lost River Bridge dispelled in a summer I shall always remember. I packed my medals in the little cardboard box with as many tragic memories as I could cram into it, and re-sealed it forever.

PART TWO

1988

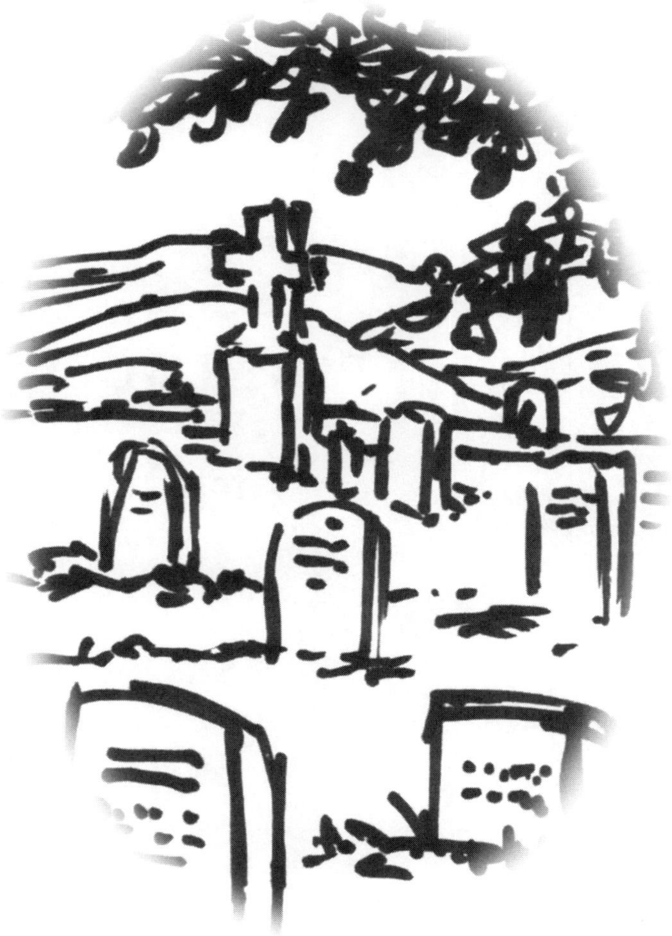

Episode Eleven

Mother Love

I returned on a Sunday morning in October after forty-two years. The memories lingered, the images clear. The turnoff remained unchanged, the road unpaved, the route unmarked. The oak and hickory canopy sheltered the twisting road, untouched by time. Goldenrod mingled with the grass overcrowding the fields at the tee intersection where wild flowers flourished the first time I passed this way. The sun cast shadows on the road to the west along the river edge and up the mountain. I smiled as I recalled my blunder taking the mountain road so many years ago. As I swung left, the bends and curves evoked a joyful anticipation. The picture of Lost River Bridge, as it was on my first visit in the summer of 1946, excited my imagination, unblemished by time. Finally, the last corner; I coasted down the hill and stopped at the intersection.

Nothing was the same. I gaped at a canvas landscape left too long in the sun, the images distorted, the colors faded. Even the bridge, the heart and soul, looked weary, worn past the stage when a coat of paint might hide its scars.

Sunday morning church started at ten thirty. Over the hill to the right and through the hollow, the church, more elegant than a picture postcard in an exotic wonderland, seemed out of place. Assorted cars and trucks, each at least five years old, some much older, waited in the parking lot where once stood hitching rails and buggies. The lot surface was concrete now. Chinese elms trimmed square on top, brushed and combed for Sunday service with not a leaf out of place, shielded the mundane view of automobiles from the serenity of the cemetery. A fieldstone path led from the parking area to the church side entrance. I walked to the front where two wrought-iron fences about twenty feet long paralleled the road and guarded the manicured lawn. A cobblestone walk led to a semicircular stone patio beneath the miniature portico supported on round columns. A black sign framed with bronze paint caught my eye. I felt a little flutter in my heart as I read the words printed in gold letters. I paused for a moment and read the sign a second time to make sure.

COMMUNITY CHURCH OF LOST RIVER BRIDGE
Reverend Emery Taber, Pastor

Morning Worship Services: Sunday 10:30 AM
Evening Vesper Services: Sunday 6:00 PM

Visitors Welcome

My heart wanted to sing. I could not hide my smile. The time was nearly eleven as I mounted the stone entrance steps and saw a gouge in the door with a dark splotch below that could be a blood stain. I entered the church. Pastor Taber stood erect in the pulpit, not bald like many Tabers. His hair was gray and full, his brows heavy above dark-rimmed glasses. The aquiline nose and curious mouth that warmed his face with happy contentment marked him as a Taber. His peppery gray-black Vandyke gave him a distinguished air enhanced by the sharp contrast with his white surplice and colorful stole. His shoulders were broad and square, projecting both physical and spiritual strength. I imagined him the image of Elijah Taber Pursey.

I took a seat in the rear behind the gray heads and slumping shoulders. He was halfway through his sermon. I could hardly believe the voice. Was this the same Emery Taber or an imposter? His manner of speech was different, and grammatically correct.

The service ended with a declaration of belief, followed by hymns and prayers. There was no choir; this congregation didn't need one. Their voices drowned out the guitar that had no amplifier. Emery marched down the aisle, a true Christian soldier, cross

LOST RIVER BRIDGE

in one hand, Bible in the other, belting out the processional in a cacophony of adoration that would wake the dead. He set his cross and Bible aside and wheeled about on the stone entrance. Irene appeared and stood on the opposite side from Emery. They greeted the parishioners in a remarkable display of joyful affection, not a single young person among them. I watched from the vestibule, the last to leave.

"Hello, Irene. Remember me?"

I hugged her, and thought she was too shocked to speak. For a moment, I regretted I had not warned them about my visit. She emitted a squeaky *oh-my-goodness* reaction, followed by a smile of recognition. I turned to Emery. I resisted the urge to put my arms around him. Instead, I took his hands in mine. He seemed unfazed by my abrupt appearance, not the least confounded. I should have known what he'd say, but his casual words caught me by surprise.

"Granny Sarah told me you'd be here today."

Our correspondence through the years had been intermittent at best; periodic Christmas cards skipped years at a time. Notices of births, marriages, and deaths begot responses of vicarious pleasure or sympathetic condolence, and always a dearth of personal news. That Emery embraced an ecclesiastic career did not surprise me. I admired his dedication to achieve it. By equal measure, my constant traipsing to remote areas of Canada building paper mills did not bring wonder to his eyes. We spent a pleasant afternoon on his front porch exchanging forty-two years of personal history.

At four o'clock, Irene wheeled a teacart through the door.

"Do you still have afternoon tea, Elijah?"

"My dear Irene, I am a Taber. Don't all Tabers have afternoon tea?"

The conversation turned to talk of her mother, Abby Watson and the day we picked the corn.

"I guess you never heard my story about love," Irene said.

I laughed. "Well, I haven't been in Lost River Bridge but a few hours, and the stories start already. No, I don't believe I've heard your tale. Please tell me."

STEPHEN P. BYERS

"I was the first-born in our family; 1928. My grandfather on my mother's side was Levi Pursey. On my father's side, my grandfather was William Watson. I like to say jealousy between the two of them caused the problem, but I'm not sure that's true. I can't tell you rightly how they came to battle for my affection. Neither one was a drinking man, tolerable I suppose, but not excessive like my Uncle Lou. Anyhow, they bribed me with gifts. Mother should have put a stop to it, but she was a new mother and maybe didn't realize what would happen.

"Sometimes they'd be at our house together, for a Sunday breakfast before church or something like that. Other times, I'd see one of them sneaking around checking if the other was about. If he saw him then he'd continue on his way as if taking some exercise with nothing on his mind. But when I was alone, he'd stop to play with me, or give me a gift; usually something small like a game he made, or maybe a candy treat, or a cookie. Neither one had much money; same as everybody else that lived here. I guess they spent what they had on me.

"I had no idea what was going on. I suppose Mama and Daddy knew, but being young parents, they probably didn't think anything about it. Probably thought it kept the old men out of mischief to visit their first grandchild. No matter, I was the center of the world for these two old men vying for my affection, taking turns playing games, bringing me toys, even feeding me. In the evenings, they'd read to me. No, that's not right. Grandpa Pursey would read to me, but Grandpa Watson told stories. I liked his stories because they were always different. He'd tell me a story about a princess, but the next time he told me the same story it was different.

"Anyway, the upshot was that everybody loved Irene and, of course, Irene loved everybody and everything, especially all the attention she attracted. It wasn't long before Irene loved Irene more than anybody else loved her.

"One day a terrible thing happened. It was the worst thing that had ever happened to Irene. At first, she didn't realize how really bad it was, but soon enough she found out. Mama went away for a few weeks. When she came home, she'd bought a live baby from

LOST RIVER BRIDGE

wherever it was she'd been. She brought it home with her and called it Timmy. Everybody wanted to look at it. All kinds of people came to the house. They wanted to hold Timmy, play with Timmy, brought toys for Timmy, even helped change Timmy's pants. Timmy. Timmy. Timmy. Both grandpas came to see Timmy in the evenings and sat swinging on the porch taking turns holding him. When they tired of that, they'd put him in the carriage and go for a walk; the two of them together laughing and talking. Seems Timmy made everybody laugh and they loved him for it. Nobody loved Irene anymore.

"A year passed. I wasn't kind to Timmy and they told me never to touch him. Everybody else could touch him so what was the matter with me? I didn't like Timmy one little bit, but that was only the start. Mama went away again for a few weeks and she bought another one. This one was called Annie. I never imagined life could get worse than it was with Timmy, but it did. I was five years old, condemned to the life of Cinderella. Irene, heat the baby's bottle. Irene, fetch this, fetch that. Irene, do this, do that. All my troubles were Annie's fault; every single one of them. Mama used to say she loved me, but I didn't believe her because soon as she said it, she'd run off to hug Annie or Timmy. For two years, no matter where we went, Daddy carried Timmy when he got tired or cried or did anything. Mummy carried Annie, but I always had to walk no matter how tired or hungry I was.

"I started school when I was six. Until the summer I was eight, I tried to stay away from home much as I could. I wasn't brave enough to run away, but I made plans to go soon as I got braver. In the summertime when school was out, I played at the homes of my friends. I told them not to come to our house because Mama and Daddy only liked little kids they could carry in their arms. They especially didn't like grown up girls that went to school.

"During that summer, the summer I was eight, the church planned a fair. We'd never had a fair before that I could remember. It was exciting with games and races and all sorts of good stuff to eat. I planned to go all day with three of my best friends. The morning of the fair, Mama spoke to me at breakfast in the kitchen.

"'Now, Irene, I want you to take Annie with you. I have to bakepies. That and looking after Timmy will keep me busy. So you take Annie and look after her.'

"'Aw, Mama! Do I have to?'

"'Yes. And don't argue. Annie, you go get ready.'

"As I watched Annie make her way to the outhouse, a wonderful idea popped into my head. As soon as she closed the door, I locked it from the outside and ran as fast as I could run.

"I don't know what happened next. I suppose Annie screamed and yelled until Mama heard her. Then, Mama didn't have a choice; she had to look after the two kids all day while I dodged about making sure Mama and Daddy couldn't find me. I had a wonderful time. Not only did I have fun playing games, but it was doubly exciting because I couldn't let Mama or Daddy see me. At five, when the fair ended and my friends went home with their families, I lost my nerve.

"Around six o'clock, I pushed open the kitchen door. Timmy was on the porch with Daddy. Annie was playing on the floor under the kitchen table.

"'Hello, Mama,' I whispered.

"'Why, Irene,' she said in her beautiful voice. 'Did you have a good time at the fair?'

"'Yes, Mama.'

"'Tell me what you did.'

"'I don't feel well. I want to go upstairs.'

"I ran to my room and closed the door. I was too confused to cry. In a little while, Mama called me.

"'Irene. Supper's ready.'

"'I'm not feeling well.'

"'I'll get the castor oil.'

"'I think I'm feeling better, now.'

"At the supper table, everybody talked about the fair. Timmy and Annie went in the afternoon with Mama. Daddy sold pies and cakes and made nearly twenty dollars for the church. Mama sold six pies, three for a dollar. Timmy won a little tooter in the fishpond. Annie bought a rag doll for ten cents. I didn't say a word.

LOST RIVER BRIDGE

"I went to my room soon as Mama said I could. Never in my life have I spent such a restless night. Sometimes, when we say we didn't sleep a wink, we really did sleep only it isn't a deep sleep and we don't feel rested in the morning. But, that night, I truly didn't sleep a wink. I couldn't understand. I was afraid, too scared to go downstairs. In the morning, when Mama called, I had to.

"'Irene! Time for breakfast.'

"The family, including grandparents, sat at the table for Sunday morning breakfast, always the best meal of the week. Mama made my favorite. She set three beautiful brown, gooey popovers covered in honey in front of me with bacon on the side.

"'Are you feeling better this morning, Irene?'

"'Yes, Daddy.'

"'Probably ate too much cotton candy, I imagine. Well, dig in! Your mother's made your favorite breakfast. Don't take too long because we'll be needing to leave for church soon.'

"I was in a terrible fix. I had to eat, but I didn't want to. I stuffed in what I could and threw the rest in the pig slop when Mama turned her back and Daddy went to hitch the carriage.

"Never have I sat through a longer church service. It usually lasted an hour and a half; this one took sixteen years. When we arrived home, I went to my room and cried all afternoon. Nobody came to see me and I knew nobody loved Irene. I was ready to kill myself. Mama called me for supper.

"'I can't come, Mama. I'm sick.'

"In a few minutes, I heard the door open. She stood at the foot of the bed. I buried my head under the pillow.

"'Do you want to tell me about it?'

"I couldn't answer.

"I heard her step into the hall. 'Call me when you're ready.' She started to close the door.

"I jumped up. 'I'm ready, Mama.' Tears poured down my face. I clung to her waiting for her to say something.

"'Tell me,' she said at last.

"'Mama! Oh! Mama. I locked Annie in the outhouse.'

"'I know that.'

"'But, you didn't say anything.'

"She pushed me back, holding me at arms length. Slowly, I raised my head to look in her eyes."

Irene had to stop her story to wipe her eyes. It took a moment before she could continue.

"Then Mama spoke the softest, most forgiving words I ever heard. She said so quiet and peaceful, 'Do I have to?'"

Irene buried her face in her handkerchief.

"Wow! Great story," I said, "and you told it so well. You never forgot, did you?"

"No, I never did."

Her voice was quiet and soft. I could not believe she had never told the story before, but then, perhaps she hadn't.

"I became close to my mother," she said as she wiped her eyes again. "Especially after we lost Daddy in the war. I felt I wanted to spend my whole life just pleasing her. More than that, I've always loved my brother and sister. It's only that when I was young, I didn't understand love."

Episode Twelve

The Beginning of the End

Irene's story created a sense of family intimacy marked by her warm expression of love. Did she tell it for a special reason? I could not explain, even to myself, why the ending surprised me. I expected something different. In retrospect, I could not imagine what. I laughed. Had I become a psychic like Emery? Impossible! Never in my life had I experienced a clairvoyant thought. Yet, I harbored a pervading sense that a secret lay hidden in her tale; Uncle Lou, perhaps. After forty-two years, how could I possibly feel guilty for threatening him? But there, you see, it sprang into my mind. Was it the sign of a guilty conscience that I should recall such an insignificant incident after so many years? Abby said I drove Lou from her house. Nonsense! If I did, where did he go? That was the ticket; track him down. Ten to one, I'd find him dead.

I drove back to the bridge consumed in thought, leaving Irene and Emery to prepare for evening service. I was about to cross when I saw a man leaning on the rail with a twig in his hand. I stopped and lowered the window.

"Hello," I said. He turned to look at me. He was middle-aged; speckled gray hair, round wide-set, steely eyes that penetrated like x-rays; a good-looking chap with an air of calmness that suggested a high level of self-confidence, or else a lot of money; maybe both.

"My name's Elijah Taber."

"Walter Applehorn."

"Oh!" I nodded towards the big house. "That your place?"

"Yes."

I opened the door, intending to shake hands, but my eye caught the river. A torrent of water flowed uphill. In places, the waves broke creating white water, while the south side flowed calmly as I remembered. I suppose the surprised look on my face was the usual reaction but I was not surprised at what he thought I was surprised at. I glanced at him.

A slight smile lit his face. "Amazing, isn't it?"

"Yes it is," I said, as I turned away for a moment. He didn't seem to know who I was, or at least he showed no sign of recognition, or curiosity. I rubbed my chin, stared at the water, and wondered how I could uncover the secret. Probably he'd have a story.

"To move the water that quickly, the tankers must be a good deal bigger than they were in forty-six."

"Tankers?"

We leaned on the rail elbow to elbow. "You don't know about the tankers?"

"No."

"Lived here long?"

"Twelve years since I came back."

"Did you know the water flowed a lot slower in forty-six?"

"I was a youngster then. Ten years old."

"And you never heard of tankers?"

"You asked me that before."

"I'm sorry. I'm thinking of something else."

We stared at the water in silence. In a few moments he said, "Funny how that water curled and formed the eddy at the weir."

"Oh!" I tried to remain casual but I think I failed to cover my surprise. "A weir, you said? In the river?"

"Yes. Sometimes in the winter when the water was low we used to walk on it."

"But you can't see it any more?"

"Not with the pump running."

"The pump?"

"Yes. I installed it."

"You installed it?"

"You sound like an echo."

"I'm sorry. I suppose you installed it as a tourist attraction?"

"Yes. In the summer it attracts lots of people. The weir never worked very well."

"I can see the pump is a big improvement." I reached out and shook his hand. "Been nice talking to you," I said. "I'm going for a drive for old time's sake."

"So long!"

The sun sank behind the western mountain, casting most homesteads in semi-darkness. A garish yellow vinyl hid the imitation brick siding I remembered on Uncle Henry's home. The place looked neat; given to one of the children probably.

Emery, you devil, you never once cracked a smile. What am I to do with you?

I didn't count as I made my depressing tour, but I sensed half the homes were empty. I imagined the local school closed fifteen or twenty years ago; the windows broken now, the door dangling on one hinge.

Emery! I'd like to wring your neck

The old folks waved as I drove slowly past; lonely people patiently waiting their time. Their children probably drag the kids from town to visit grandpa and grandma on holidays. An event, no doubt, that serves to remind parents how grateful they are to live elsewhere.

I returned across the bridge. Walter was nowhere in sight. I stopped to check the river once more. Not a ripple marred the surface. As near as I could see in the dark, from side to side it flowed downhill like every other stream in the world. Shut the pump at night and save electricity, I guessed.

Emery! You're a corker.

I drove past the Emporium, a sad sight. The shattered glass of the rusty hand-operated gas pumps bespoke a sorry epitaph. I turned at the bend where the road leads to the mountain. Doc Schumacher lived up that road. I never did meet them, but I guessed I'd find out soon enough what became of them.

Outdoor lights illuminated a sign at the Applehorn place. I wondered what kind of perseverance it took to get the long-time residents to assent to such a bold symbol of commercialism.

LOST RIVER BED AND BREAKFAST — CABINS
Fireside Café
Walter & Eloise Applehorn, Owners

A white flickering neon sign signaled a vacancy. Cars parked in the lot where the meeting hall once stood. I walked around the lot to search the area behind the remains of the stone foundation. In the darkness, I slid one foot ahead, then the other, swinging them in wide arcs. My right foot hit, rather more forcibly than I intended. The horseshoe pitch! The bench where Abby and I talked must have been about there.

Beside the restaurant entrance, crimson neon letters announced The Fireside Café was open. I pushed the door and stepped inside. A woman served tables. She signaled. I waited. I guessed between forty-five and fifty. Pretty face, stubby legs, blond ponytail pulled through the opening in the back of a red baseball cap. I could not make out the name. Then I realized it was script at an angle. As she came towards me, I read Chiefs beside an arrowhead image. She greeted me. Her name; Eloise Applehorn.

"Passing through," I said. "Maybe a week, ten days. Who knows; maybe a month or more. Could you put me up?"

"No problem."

We agreed on a price. I signed the register.

"Oh! Elijah Taber! Are you related to Emery?"

"Distantly, yes."

She agreed to chat when the guests departed after dinner. Meanwhile, I ordered supper, and helped take the dishes to the kitchen afterwards. In the informal atmosphere, she appreciated guests helping. We rinsed and stacked the washer. She finished in the kitchen while I wiped the tables, and put the condiments in place. She entered with a tray of coffee, switched off the open sign, smiled, and said, "I always forget that thing. Let's talk."

"There are so many questions I want to ask, I don't know where to begin."

Her warm smile encouraged me, perhaps with a little sympathy although she couldn't possibly know about Emery's tanker tale.

"Did you say you came here in 1946?"

"Yes," I said as I poured coffee. "Would you tell me the story about the Bed and Breakfast? I confess when I arrived this morning, the sight of the signs startled me."

This was her story.

"My husband, Walter, is Abner's grandson. He was ten years old in forty-six; a child living among the many you probably never noticed in this house. His father sent him away to school. He studied petroleum engineering. Went into the oil business—wildcat drilling—made lots of money. He believes in easy come, easy go and the only way to stop the go is to quit when you're ahead. He retired at the age of thirty-six with enough money to live comfortably for the rest of his life and lots left over to play with.

"We didn't have children, still don't and never will have. I followed him wherever he went. He was my man and I wasn't letting him out of my sight. I ran the mess hall and did the cooking. When he decided to quit, I told him I wanted my own little restaurant some place. He said he knew just the spot. He bought this house.

"Walter never served in the armed forces. He didn't have merit badges, either, playing in a rough league, as he did. But the folks here regarded him as a hero just the same because he came back to make Lost River Bridge his home. Everybody knew he had money. I believe that isn't why they welcomed him. He was an Applehorn, Abner's grandson, and that was enough to make them love him.

"We hadn't been here but a few weeks when we learned three of the boys from here—the youngest Hubblewaite boy, George Fuller and Andy Harper—didn't come back from Vietnam. The families had organized a group to build a monument with the names of the war-dead chiseled in native stone. Everybody contributed but they still didn't have enough. Walter made it possible. A dedication ceremony took place on November 11. The whole place stopped work for a few minutes to remember the fallen. The next year most folks forgot the memorial on Veteran's Day. Emery Taber was furious. Without consultation, he changed forever the tradition of Remembrance Day at Lost River Bridge.

"He and Father Lalonde, from the Catholic Church down Gainesville way, arranged a service on the Sunday nearest Veteran's Day. Regular meeting time for Mass was eight-thirty and the Community Church service was at ten thirty, so they agreed to meet by the bridge at two-thirty with the parishioners from both churches. They accepted no excuses for absenteeism except if you were on your deathbed. Two or three years after they began this tradition, it snowed; a wet, miserable snow and most everybody stayed home. Emery considered that unbefitting. He succeeded in working Father Lalonde into a rage equal to his own. Through the rest of November and on into December, you wouldn't believe how the two of them scolded their parishioners with sermons about the victims of war. Most folks weren't sure what the fuss was about but they accepted the scolding with humility, as they always do. The prelates cooled down by Advent. In the spirit of Christmas, they forgave their flocks for ingratitude to those that gave their lives in honor.

"Folks remembered those harsh sermons. As so often happens, having fallen on their faces in humiliation, they toppled over backwards in remorse. The following year notices of the ten o'clock service at the cenotaph at Lost River Bridge appeared in newspapers as far away as Rolla, Jefferson City and Springfield. A few folks from the cities came down to pay their respects, especially since the hunting season happened to be open; might bag a deer or a wild turkey. Every year more and more hunters trooped down this way leaving their wives and children to attend the service as they headed to the woods for a day of hunting. The reaction from the locals ranged from outright hostility to threats of uprising.

"Walter, who is, to say the least, an extremely enterprising guy, had been trying to figure out how he could get away with opening a motel, a bed and breakfast and my restaurant without everybody running us out of town. He had an idea. He invited the town folks to meet on the front porch of this house. With maybe a hundred people milling about, he managed to direct the discussion to stopping *them furriners* coming to the Remembrance Day Service. Suggestions ranged from road barricades to shooting on sight.

LOST RIVER BRIDGE

"Walter bided his time. When the conversation subsided a little, he took his turn. 'Why do you want to stop them?'

"Well, you never heard the likes. Folks soared into a tirade Bessie said she could hear all the way down at the Emporium.

"'Good Lord, Walter,' somebody yelled. 'Where you been, Son? Them *furriners* make a mess of everything they touch. They scare the animals in the pasture, hunt quail in the cornfields, start fires in the woods and trample the ground in the pig sties.'

"This sounded to Walter like the behavior of about half the residents of Lost River Bridge. He was wise enough to keep his mouth shut, letting them rant about paper lunch bags, cardboard cups and empty beer bottles.

"One of the old men started lecturing. 'Years ago when your granddaddy was a boy, Walter, thar weren't no questions asked. Him and his pals chased 'em *furriners* to the woods and thet was thet. When I was a boy, the law was agin us. What we done was fire over ter heads. Weren't many *furriners* hanging round when we got done with chasing 'em. No siree.' The old man's eyes went heavenward with a prayerful gleam for days gone by.

"Then another spoke up. 'You know who's to blame, Walter? It's Henry Ford; that's who; him and 'em dang cars of hisen. What gives 'em *furriners* the right to drive 'em cars round our town? Tell me thet, huh!'

"Walter laughed when he told me later not one of them remembered no person ever lived in Ozark County who loved automobiles more than Abner. Hearing these fellows cuss out Ford was like hearing Wyatt Earp cuss out Colt Manufacturing.

"'Now hold on there,' Walter said. 'They got money, haven't they?'

"Curious heads turned. 'Well, I don't know. I suppose they do,' somebody said.

"'Sure they do' said Walter. 'They drive fancy cars and pickup trucks that don't come cheap.'

"'Thet's right. Got fancy guns, too.'

"When they finished assessing the value of the *furriner's* possessions, you might have thought the subject was the Rockefellers.

"'Well,' Walter said, 'if they have so much money, surely they'd be happy to share it with us poor mountain folk.'

"The puzzled faces fell silent. A few moments passed before Mr. Hubblewaite corralled his senses. 'Wait a minute. Walter! How we going to do that?'

"Walter climbed up on a chair and put his hands above his head like a presidential candidate accepting the nomination and said, 'I'm going to make this house a tourist home.'

"The aura of surprise suppressed the void of incomprehension. Silence reigned as mouths gaped and eyes bugged. Some staggered backwards, clutching the veranda rail. Others turned their backs. Two or three started down the steps. I saw a man and woman staring at each other, motionless as if Walter had said he planned to build an atomic power plant on the river.

"Reggie Hooper recovered first. 'What'd you say?'

"Walter shrugged. 'They've got money, don't they?'

"Three weeks passed before the reaction subsided. Some people suggested Walter experienced a blow to the head when drilling for oil. Some thought he injured his brain when he fell from a tree as a child. His old school teacher remembered behavioral problems. Sunday gatherings after church produced various proposals from asking Walter to leave town to asking the state legislature to pass a law.

"Emery undertook to look into the matter. 'That'll be the subject of my sermon next Sunday,' he announced.

"True to his word, he delivered his sermon to the congregation that overflowed the church. He started with, 'Do not judge lest you be judged,' and ended with, 'What you do to the least of them, you do unto to Me.' The congregation sat in astonishment.

"'Walter's suggestion ignites the true Christian spirit.' Emery paused. He lowered his voice scarcely above a whisper. 'And I don't think twenty cents a night plus five cents for the Community Church Improvement Fund is too much to ask for a night in our campground.'

"Walter looked puzzled. After the service, he said to Emery, 'Our campground?'

"Emery shook his hand. 'Thank you, Walter. I knew you'd understand.'"

"Eloise," I asked, "where did you come from?"
"Oklahoma."
"Just wondered. You tell a story like an Ozark native."
She laughed and filled the coffee cups. "It's going on twelve years I've lived in this house, ten of them running this café. You can't listen to these old codgers coming in here spinning their yarns day after day and not learn how to tell."
I had not steered the conversation but suddenly the perfect opportunity arose. "Did you ever hear tell of Lou Pursey?"
She looked puzzled. "No," she said. "That's not a familiar name." After a momentary pause, she added, "In fact, I don't think there is any family of that name here now."
"Irene's mother, Abby, was a Pursey. She had a brother, Lou, who had a bad time in World War Two. Drank heavily, couldn't face reality. Doc Schumacher and his wife Gerda took him in. That was in forty-six, the summer I spent here."
"How old would Lou be now?"
"Let's see. I remember he was two or three years older than me. That'd make him sixty-eight. Something like that."
Eloise rose, put the cups on the tray and carried it through to the kitchen. I wasn't sure, but I thought I heard her mumble the word *strange*. I went to the kitchen. She had rinsed the coffee service and was putting away the dishes from the washer. I joined her, itching to ask what was on her mind. Obviously, the conversation about Lou triggered something. We finished the chore in silence.
"I better get my bags from the car," I said. She had a faraway look on her face and I thought she hadn't heard me. Before I could repeat myself, she put her hand on my forearm. She spoke in a subdued tone as if absorbed in a riddle.
"Strange. I don't suppose there is any connection but people talk about a hermit living in the woods around here. They call him Jack Polecat. I don't know what that means."
"I do," I said.

Episode Thirteen

Deceit

I don't believe a day passed after I registered at the Bed and Breakfast before everybody knew about me. Eloise said she reminded, "Well, maybe one or two folks about your visit in 1946." I imagined not one customer came into the café and said good morning before she spilled the news about my return.

The community accepted Eloise as if born and raised there, probably because she wore the name Applehorn so proudly. They regarded her as a sort of Joan of Arc based on several whispered accounts. "We shouldn't be talking about her but did you know she received guidance from Saint Michael?" Despite her nearly fifty years, they labeled her "a sweet child." She reveled in the talk. "Imagine what Walter woulda done if it ain't been for Eloise." She did little to discourage it. Had there been a telephone exchange, Eloise would have been the operator, or the postmaster, if they had a post office.

Once recalled by whatever means, the stories about me magnified into unbelievable incidents. "You must be the boy them French fellows shot over to the Bellechase place in the hills. Where was you wounded?" Several versions of the experience circulated. Two people asked, "Was you the same furriner what dug the foxhole at the sawmill." Somebody else wanted to know, "How long did you serve in jail for counterfeiting?"

As a resident of the Bed and Breakfast, I chatted with the early eaters and the coffee drinkers in the mornings. Like Eloise, I did nothing to discourage the talk. In fact, I threw in a few details to improve the stories with the thought perhaps I might add a foot or two to the length of the snakes. I encouraged the myths and devoted my days to Emery and Irene.

Even with a decreasing congregation, Emery had found money over the years for continuing church maintenance and improvements. Irene contributed whole-hearted support, organizing various fund-raising events that produced plenty of goodwill, comradeship and discarded clothing, but little money.

Hooking to Walter's coattails proved to be a wise move. Walter agreed to a seven-percent surcharge on rooms, cabins and camping in exchange for supervision of the gardens at the Bed and Breakfast, which became the center of activity soon after the conversion.

When the breakfast-eaters left the café for their various jobs, I shuffled along to the church. On my way, I often thought about Emery's tenacity. I remembered our days toiling and talking in the cemetery when he told me his dreams. He succeeded more than he failed. As only the second resident pastor—a goal he never mentioned in the old days—the community respected and admired him. One dream remained unaccomplished; no bell tower and spire capped the church. On Sundays, he played a recording over a loudspeaker but the sound of a real church bell remained beyond his grasp. He told me he felt unrewarded as if his need for a church bell dwarfed everything he had modernized in fifty years of dedicated service. I thought how remarkable he could strive ever onward with exciting dreams while praise for his accomplishments embarrassed him.

I caught sight of him in bib overalls as I reached the church. Back and forth he went pushing the mower and plucking weeds.

"That the same pair of overalls you wore forty years ago?"

"Yep," he said, smiling in a manner that was new to me. Where he had been shy and reticent in his youth, now he took charge of his emotions instead of the other way around.

"Got another mower?"

"Nope, but you can have this one."

He disappeared inside the church. I mowed for an hour. When he came out, he suggested we relax on the porch. He didn't need to ask me twice. Irene joined us, bringing lemonade.

"Had a delightful talk with Eloise last evening," I said.

Irene, with occasional interjections from Emery, told her version of the events leading to Walter's various enterprises. The stories were similar except Emery claimed Walter suggested the surcharge to support the church claiming he, Emery, never would have had the courage to suggest such an arrangement.

Despite my hopes the story of Lou would flow naturally into our conversation, it never arose. I tried a different approach.

"Irene, tell me about Annie and Timmy."

She offered a weak smile. Her eyes shifted as if seeking to avoid a subject she didn't want to discuss. A forlorn sigh conceded resignation that she could not shield herself from the pain my question delivered. She looked away, then cast her eyes on the floor. At last, she mumbled an answer.

"Poor Annie. Too impulsive. Divorced, I'm afraid. Lives in Fayetteville with her daughter. They both teach school."

I regretted opening such a sad bag of woes and hoped her brother fared better.

"And Timmy?"

She brightened as if relieved that I did not probe further into Annie's circumstances.

"First of all, he hates people calling him Timmy. It's some queer notion he has about respect for Daddy. His name, he announces in superior tones, is Timothy in honor of his father. With any encouragement at all, he launches into a story of Father's war record, which I fear may not be quite accurate." This last thought brought a smile to her lips. I recalled her saying when Timmy came into the household everybody loved him. I thought at the time that her comments reflected her own jealousy, but now the inference was that Timmy did indeed have an engaging personality.

"Ah! An Ozark storyteller! And what does he do for a living?"

"He teaches geology. His students love him. One of those old-time professors in corduroy jacket burned with pipe ash. You went to college, I'm sure you know the type. Mother worked hard to pay for his education. He helped by winning scholarships and paid for all his postgraduate studies himself. Then, when he got the university appointment, he repaid Mother by supporting her in a home."

"Sounds like a real success story."

She nodded her agreement, I judged recovered from the pain of reciting Annie's problems. I decided to take the plunge, unprepared for the reaction.

"What about your Uncle Lou?"

The words no sooner left my mouth than Emery rose.

"Excuse me," he said, glaring at me with what amounted to a vicious snarl. He marched down the steps towards the church. Irene watched him go and heaved a heavy sign.

"You shouldn't have asked."

"I'm sorry. I never imagined it was such a touchy subject. Could you tell me why? I mean, would it help, maybe, if you talked about it?"

She sighed again.

"I suppose, but not if Emery is around."

"Please tell me the story."

"For a long time after Lou left, Mother blamed you. I tried to persuade her life would be easier with him away. He was messing up her life and ours; I mean Annie, Timothy and me. I think she saw it my way before she died mostly because of Timothy's success. She was so proud of him and Lou hanging around could easily have steered Timothy in the wrong direction. In many ways, Timothy was so gullible. I think Mother realized that and agreed with me that we would be better off without Lou in our house. I knew it hurt her to suggest to him that he leave. I guess her choice was between him and her children. I'm grateful she chose us.

"Anyway, Lou arranged to live with Doc and Gerda. He worked for his keep. They persuaded him to quit drinking and he became a good gardener. Grew vegetables, had a little orchard, did canning, that sort of thing. He never had animals, probably because Gerda never could have stood the mess and stink they make. Naturally, his recovery pleased Mama; justified what she had done.

"It didn't last too long. Let's see—1968, I think—Gerda died. She was a big woman who worked too hard and ate too much. One day her heart gave up trying; she collapsed and died ten minutes later. That would be twenty years ago. Doesn't seem that long somehow. Without her, Doc fell to pieces and dragged Lou with him. They took to drinking. The medical services stopped. Wasn't anything we could do. Those two men lived alone in dirt and filth. It was awful.

"Sloppy and drunk half the time, the inevitable happened. In the winter of seventy-three the house caught fire. Doc died in the blaze; probably passed out, unable to escape. Lou wasn't hurt. At least he never admitted to me he was. I used to see him once in a while. Because Emery carried such hard feelings, I couldn't ask Lou here. I'd make excuses that I needed to get something in town. 'Nothing serious,' I'd say to Emery. 'Sore throat or headache or something.' I'd spend the time talking with Lou, always scared to death Emery would find out. In a place like this where everybody knows everybody else's business, we had to arrange a special meeting place where nobody would see us. I hated it; I mean being so deceitful with my own husband. I'd come back and try to explain to Emery without telling him where I'd really been. 'It isn't Christian,' I'd say, but he plain wouldn't listen. I couldn't go on so I had to stop trying to meet with Lou. It's so sad. I tried, honest, Elijah, I tried but I couldn't ... ." Her voice trailed off and the story ended.

"A sad tale," I said, "but why is Emery upset?"

"You won't believe this, Elijah. It's because of a stupid medallion that Emery says Lou stole and Emery wants it. Elijah, I love Emery. I've loved him ever since I was a little girl. He is a wonderful Christian man, takes nothing for himself, gives whatever he has; you couldn't ask for a kinder, dearer soul. The only thing that ever stood between him and me is the crazy notion he has about Granny Sarah's medallion. You saw for yourself; soon as the subject arose, he ups and leaves. Won't even talk about it any more. For the life of me, as Christian as he is, I can't understand why he won't forgive Lou who hasn't done anything to Emery."

I took her hand. "I'm sorry. I didn't mean—"

"It's okay." She looked at me with a half smile. "It's not your fault."

Having delved this far into the mystery, with a reluctant shrug, I decided to keep going.

"Did you know I made a rubbing of the imprint left by the medallion in the back of your family Bible?"

"No. Tell me."

I related the story, ending with Emery's intuitive remark. Her face clouded into a puzzled frown.

"Annie never forgave me for locking her in the outhouse. I've apologized a hundred times but she won't give in. It never occurred to me until this minute, it's because of the medallion. I'll bet she took that letter and hid it."

"Irene, I'm sorry. I'm afraid I've dug into personal information you'd rather not talk about." I wasn't going to tell her, but I made up my mind I'd go to Fayetteville and find Annie. I guessed I was butting in where I probably shouldn't, but something gnawed at me, pushing me on against my will and certainly against my better judgment. I was close to the secret she harbored in her heart. Every line in her face, the intermittent dabbing at her eyes and the drawn lips, shouted her need to confess. I'd seen it the day before in her story of love and now, try as she might, she could not hide it. Something about Lou condemned her to a personal purgatory, something I wanted her to tell me, not for my sake but for hers.

"No, it's not like that," she said. "I know you mean well. But, it's difficult. I don't know what to say."

"You've never heard a single word from Lou in the last ten years or more?"

Her reaction was as if I touched a nerve. Her head jerked in both directions. I thought at first she detected a noise, an animal or something. As the color rose in her cheeks, I realized she looked to see if Emery was anywhere in sight. She stood and took my hand. "Let's go inside," she said.

She pulled a chair close to mine at the kitchen table. Her voice was low. I had to lean close to distinguish words that came between soft gasps for air as if she choked.

"People say the Schumacher house is haunted." She paused between every sentence. I waited as she struggled and stammered trying to say the words aloud. "I believe Lou lives there. If not in the house, then nearby in the woods." Her eyes were wide with a mixture of fear and awe that I couldn't read. She put her lips almost to my ear. "Promise you won't tell Emery."

"Tell him what?"

"Promise!"

"Okay. I promise."

She rose from the table, looked through the kitchen door to the front room and closed it without a sound. She drew back the curtain at the kitchen window, looked across to the church and pulled down the roller blind. Apparently satisfied we were alone, she sank into the chair beside me in the darkened kitchen. As before, we sat close together, her mouth near my ear. Her voice, less edgy made me think she had recovered a little confidence, whether from knowing Emery was busy elsewhere or simply that she had prepared herself to confess, I do not know.

"Once a week, I put food out behind the woodshed. Canned goods, perishable stuff I put in tins. I put it in a burlap sack. It's always gone in the morning. There's an empty sack left behind. I number them so I know the one that's left is different from the one I put the food in." I turned to see her face. She choked back the tears filling her eyes. "I feel awful."

"Why?" I held her hand and waited an eternity for her answer.

"Because ... because I'm deceiving Emery."

Later, as we drank our usual afternoon tea on the porch with Emery, she was quite jovial. We talked around a wide range of topics. I learned for the first time that Walter bought abandoned homes and had a standing offer to buy any house from a family moving elsewhere. I wondered why. Irene and Emery didn't know.

Episode Fourteen

The Truth about Doc

In mid-week, the weather turned bad. Severe thunder, lightning, torrential downpour, and intermittent high winds continued through the night. I heard the rumble as I pushed open the dining room door and stepped into the café for breakfast. People crowded elbow to elbow like frenzied farmers at a livestock auction.

In one corner, a card game involved frantic betting, and cautious indecision that produced outbursts I thought would end in a fistfight. Seven players rebuked one another for playing too fast, playing too slow, playing the wrong card, and even playing at all in a game too serious for jovial conviviality. A large hand thumped a card down with a shout of victory. The winner swept the pile of matchsticks from the center of the table amid a barrage of insults accompanied by curses, and slurs about stupidity and blind luck.

In an equally emotional scene on the other side of the dining room, a crowd of kibitzers groaned and cheered the progress of three checker games. They shouted instructions and epithets offering bets like Las Vegas gamblers. The big players plunked down as much as a nickel, most limited their wagers to a penny, and a few played for tokens of one sort and another.

"Nobody's going to work in this storm," Eloise said as I gave her my order for breakfast.

"I suppose, but why is everybody here on a day like this? Why aren't they at home?"

"Power's down."

"You seem to have plenty of power."

"That's why they're here. We're the only ones with a generator." She smiled and winked. "My best days are storm days."

I carried my plate to the card players and pulled a chair close to watch the shenanigans while I ate.

"Hey, you guys! Make room for Elijah. Want a hand?"

"The stakes are pretty high for me," I said.

I spent the morning helping in the kitchen, made coffee and filled cups. The storm eased around ten and the power came on a few minutes after eleven. The games broke up and folks headed for home. Some had been there since five, but Eloise knew what each owed. Although she kept the process simple—breakfast two and a quarter, coffee fifty cents—still she knew who ate and who didn't. She punched the cash register every third or fourth customer, the rest went into her pocket.

"Won't be anybody here for lunch," she said as the last one left. "Want a sandwich?"

"Sure. How about a BLT?"

"No. Don't have any bacon. Grilled cheese and tomato soup."

She was right; only the two of us for lunch, which she prepared while I wiped the tables. When she carried in the tray, she brought three servings.

"Walter will be along soon," she said

The words hardly escaped her before he barged in. "Some storm," he said looking like a deep-sea fisherman as he pulled off his knee-high boots and unclipped his yellow sou'wester outfit.

"Bridge was creaking and shaking something awful. I'm starved." He gulped a spoonful of soup and bit into his sandwich. "I thought she was coming down for sure this time."

"Is it that bad?"

Down went two or three spoonfuls of soup and the rest of the sandwich. "Yes, sir. You better believe it. You know, when that bridge goes, it'll be the end of this place."

Eloise started to laugh. "Come on, Walter. You're always saying dumb things like that. You're as bad as Andy Harper with all your doom and gloom."

LOST RIVER BRIDGE

It was Walter's turn to laugh. "That sure was funny when old man Harper got all riled up about the Doc. I've never seen anything as funny, except the time I told everybody I was going to build tourist cabins and open a restaurant."

"Tell Elijah about the doctor meeting while I get you some more soup. Another sandwich?"

"Please," Walter said, "if you don't mind."

He cleared his throat to began his story.

"Soon after we opened this place, it became sort of a town meeting hall that replaced the old building across the road that collapsed one winter. Summer of seventy-eight, I guess, six months after the fire that killed Doc, Andy Harper started making a fuss about somebody to replace Schumacher. I shouldn't make fun of old Andy. He nearly went crazy when he lost his boy in Vietnam. I remember when I was a kid, he was grumpy then, but losing your only boy in a stupid war that was none of our business, I guess maybe that's enough to put anybody off his feed.

"Seems like Mrs. Harper came down with something. Andy had to take her to Gainesville. He bellyached to everybody like he always does about everything. This time he complained he wasted a whole day. Fact is, if he hadn't wasted the day looking after her he'd have wasted it doing something else. If Eloise were here, she'd tell me I shouldn't say things like that. She's right. Anyway, here he was in the Fireside Café bellowing the blues telling folks in one form or another, 'We got to do something 'bout it.'

"Of course, everybody ignored old Andy blowing his stack again. So what else is new? But he was serious and didn't leave off this time. He talked it up in church, he talked it up on the front porch of the Emporium, and he talked it up here in this room.

"The constant yakking got people teed off a little. Finally, Mr. Fuller, nicest guy you ever want to meet—lost a boy in Vietnam too—got fed up and told Andy to either put up or shut up. Andy surprised the world by organizing a meeting. Took place right here in this room. Seems like every man, woman, and child within ten miles came. Eloise pushed back the tables, and a bunch of us brought the old meeting hall benches from the storage shed in back of the Emporium. Must have been well over a hundred people crammed in here.

"As near as anybody could make out, Andy's wife was on her deathbed with a heart condition that would do her in. Andy cranked up the truck, bedded her down best he could and took her into Gainesville. She made a rapid recovery. They were back by two in the afternoon with Andy hopping mad. He figured if Herman Schumacher had been alive, he'd have taken her there or Doc would have come over to Andy's place and found out she wasn't sick one bit except for a little stomach gas. As it was, he'd shot the morning and half the afternoon, and he'd had to buy gas to boot.

"Andy praised the virtues of Herman Schumacher, and his wife Gerda who assisted at the birth of the children of near everybody present. The more he talked, the more he got carried away with his own words. I suppose there was a mite of truth in what he said, but it sounded pretty funny."

Walter rose from the table, hitched up his pants and swaggered to the front playing the part of Andy Harper in a southern drawl I couldn't hope to imitate.

"'Now y'all listen heah, folks! Herman Schumacher was a good man. He done looked after snakebites, broken limbs, upset tummies, childbirth and everythin' in between. Ain't anybody heah in this room didn't know thar weren't much thet Herman and Gerda didn't know 'bout doct'rin'. More 'n thet, he had the good sense to know what he didn't know. Y'all know he'd tell you he didn't know but maybe Gerda would know. He saw to it folks went to the hospital right off. Now, y'all know that's the sign of a good doctor. Not too proud to say thar warn't thin's he don't know.'

Eloise came in with a bowl of soup and another sandwich, her head turning this way and that. "Gosh," she said, "I thought Andy Harper was here." Walter sat down at the table and started into his soup and sandwich. "You finish the story, Eloise."

"Where were you at?"

"When old Jim Custer got into the act."

"I remember," she said as she filled her coffee cup and mine, then settled in to finish the story.

LOST RIVER BRIDGE

"Jim Custer lives up the hill on the Booneville Road. When he heard Andy saying all these wonderful things about Doc, he hollered, 'Maybe so but he sure was a miserable cuss.'

"That set old Andy on fire. 'Just a minute,' he snorted. 'Who said that?'

"Jim stood and said, "I did, and what you going to do about it?"

"'I'm agoing to say you know you ain't got no right to talk trash that-a-way,' screamed Andy. 'I'm agoing to say you know better than to cuss out Doc. I'm agoing to say when you caught your leg in the bear trap, Schumacher tended you and you didn't get no gangrene. Ain't thet true?'

"'Well, yeah. I guess so.' Old Jim sank into his chair while a smile spread across Andy's face.

"'Then you ain't got no call to say nothing contrary.'

"A chorus of objections rose. Most agreed Doc had done good work looking after them, but it was his attitude that annoyed people. The truth is that Doc Schumacher never seemed to be happy. Maybe it was Gerda who was so work oriented and so compulsive a cleaner she drove him crazy. He seldom had a pleasant word.

"'Now y'all wait justa minute,' Andy said, banging the table with his fist. 'I didn't ask you heah to hang Schumacher no more then to call him no saint. I asked y'all to this heah meetin' on accounta we need 'nother doctor. It don't matter none if'n you liked Herman and Gerda or ya didn't, y'all got to admit sure was mighty handy when they was heah.'

"'Well, how we going to do that?' It was Bear-trap Jim on his feet again. 'There ain't more 'n 'bout a hundred souls in this whole place and more leaving every day. Ain't a doctor alive what's going to move to a place like this, leastwise not one that's any good.'

"That kind of quieted the crowd as neighbors whispered to one another. Suddenly a voice boomed from the rear of the hall.

"'So you all think Schumacher was a saint and a devil. You're praising him in one breath and cussing him in the next.'

"Sheriff Wilbur Mackay stood in the doorway, thumbs hooked into his belt, hat pushed back and his service revolver at his side.

Wilbur was getting on in years. Less than a year later he died. Andy, standing up at the front of the room, looked as perplexed as anyone.

"'You got somethin' to say, Sheriff?'

"Wilbur strode down the aisle and faced the crowd. 'Before you folks get all het up over something you cain't do nothing 'bout, you better understand that Herman Schumacher was closer to a devil than he were to a saint.'

"Silence fell. As usual, Andy recovered first. 'Whatcha mean, Sheriff?'

"'Anybody remember when Schumacher first came here?'

"A few hands raised as a rumble circulated. The sheriff glared around the room. I'll say one thing for Wilbur, he was a natural born actor. His timing was always perfect. He waited, hands on hips, until the whole crowd pleaded with him. 'Tell us, sheriff. Tell us a story. We probably heard it before but tell us again.'

"Wilbur began his tale.

"'I guess folks what might 'member is either too old to 'tend this here meeting or they're dead. It happened long 'fore my time in this county, and I ain't never had cause to do nothing 'bout it. Most of you know Lizzie Taber was Lizzie Applehorn 'fore she married Henry Taber. About 1910, just a few weeks 'fore Lizzie Applehorn came into this world, her mother took sick. Abner rushed her to the hospital. He swore he'd see to it such a thing would never happened again. He said he'd personally find a doctor to work here in Lost River Bridge. It took a while but true to his word, 'fore he died, he arranged for Schumacher to come here.'

"'Thet don't make no difference, Sheriff,' Andy said. 'We all know Mr. Applehorn provided fer Lost River Bridge. Like him or not, we want 'nother doctor like Schumacher.'

"The Sheriff smirked as he surveyed the people. 'Yeah. Y'all want another one just like old man Herman. Let's have a show of hands. If Herman climbed out of his grave and walked in through that door, how many of you would welcome him back?'

"Several hands shot up. A murmur filled the air and gradually more hands showed.

LOST RIVER BRIDGE

"'Well,' Mackay said, 'I'd say leastwise three quarters of you. But afore you cast your votes, I'm gonna ask y'all a question. Schumacher lived here for a mighty long time. Does any of you know, or can any of you guess, why a doctor with a wife who knew a bunch 'bout medicine would want to live in the backwoods? I mean if he's as good as y'all say, he'd want to work in a big hospital somewhere. Think 'bout it! Wouldn't he want to be with other medical hotshots who'd recognize his fame and all that stuff?'

"When Andy called the meeting, he never suspected this development. He sensed he was about to lose. 'Now, Sheriff, we don't need to get all het up 'bout thet. We ain't heah for to discuss the past. We want to talk—'

"'Sit down and shut up, Harper!' Bear-trap Jim was hollering and waving his hat in the air. 'Let the Sheriff speak.'

A brief round of applause followed. Andy sat.

"'All right,' said Wilbur, 'I'll answer my own question.' He placed his hat on the table in front of Andy, hitched his trousers and turned to the onlookers. 'The answer is no doctor would ever come to a place like this to work.' He gazed around the silent room waiting for his message to sink in. Finally, Bear-trap Jim rose once more.

"'You telling us Schumacher weren't no doctor?'

"'That's what I'm telling you.'

"As Brunhilde Draper leaped to her feet, the string of her bonnet caught in the chair. Her hat pulled sideways, making her appear to be screeching through her ear. 'You mean that man touched my ... .' She pulled her bonnet straight. 'I mean he felt my ... .' Her horrified face drained to ashen white. 'I mean he weren't no doctor!'

"Elijah, you never saw anything like it. Every one of the women was thinking the same as Brunhilde. They were stunned. The men roared with laughter. During the turmoil, the sheriff never moved and never smiled. He stood there until they settled down.

"'Brunhilde,' he said when the crowd quieted, 'I don't know what he touched and what he felt. I'm only telling you he wasn't no doctor.'

"'Well, carnsarn it, what was he?'

"The sheriff stepped forward letting his eyes survey the room. 'He was an orderly in a hospital in a German settlement in Canada during the first World War. It's called Kitchener today, but afore the Great War in fourteen it was called Berlin. Abner promised to bring a doctor to town. He couldn't find one and being as how he was a man of his word, he paid Schumacher money—I don't know how much but I'm guessing it was a bunch—to play the part. I'll wager Schumacher was mighty happy to oblige afore them Canadians lynched him or whatever they do up there to them what they don't like. When Abner come back, he built the house on the hill. That's how I found out what was going on. I checked the records in the county office. Sure enough, Abner owned the house. I went to see him 'bout it. He talked me into keeping my mouth shut. I went to see Gerda and Herman to let them know that I was wise to what was going on. I told them if they ever so much as harmed a single person round here, they'd be swinging from a white oak tree in Canada afore they knew what hit them. I found out Gerda had gone to doctoring school. She knew a bunch of medical magic, all right. That's why Herman consulted her all the time. She wasn't going to let him undertake nothing she couldn't handle. I watched them real close over the years. I figured they did a lot more good than harm, so I didn't tell nobody.'

"The murmuring died down after a few minutes. Emery Taber, who you know is Abner's grandson, walked to the front, faced the sheriff and began his slow drawl.

"'There ain't never been a more respected man ever lived in this place than Abner Applehorn. I think you're telling us that ain't true. You're telling us he was a scoundrel. Sheriff, I take umbrage at them words.'

"Fearing the confrontation might come to blows, Walter stepped between the two men. 'Wait a minute boys,' he said. 'Emery you go back to your seat. Sheriff you sit down over there.'

"Walter faced the audience. 'Abner was my granddad, too. You know he always did what was best for this place and doctor or no doctor, Herman and Gerda Schumacher were good for this town.

But, like someone said a while back, we can't expect a doctor to open an office in Lost River Bridge. So here's what I'm willing to do. I'll set aside a room in the Bed and Breakfast for a medical office. We'll find a doctor in one of the nearby cities that's willing to come here one day a week. Since he won't be paying rent, I expect it'll be an attractive proposition.'"

We carried our coffee to the back veranda that at one time extended the full width of the house. Now, a first aid room occupied half the space. The door had a large red cross above a sign saying the hours were Friday ten to five. It gave an emergency telephone number and a note to call the hospital in Mountain Home if that failed. A pay telephone hung on the wall.

"Walter," I said, "you're like your grandfather. You're good for this place."

Episode Fifteen

Annie

On Saturday afternoon of the following week, as I drove to Fayetteville to find Annie, I pondered my decision to live in Lost River Bridge. After years in the backwoods of Canada, the solitude of the rivers and mountains lost none of their allure for me. I intended to enjoy my new home to the fullest. I had no regrets when I left Canada except for the winter season, which was an exhilarating time for me. As a child, I loved winter sports. As an adult, I found few activities as stimulating as tromping through the woods on snowshoes, but I was prepared to sacrifice the cold weather and throw my snow blower away.

Irene had given me Annie's married name and address. I wrote to ask if I might visit at her convenience. When I rang the doorbell, a large woman with short curly hair, blue eyes and a pretty smile, opened the door.

"Annie Jamieson?"

"Yes."

"My name is Elijah Taber."

She ushered me into a room with two reclining chairs that faced a television set. Eating utensils on end tables beside each chair suggested meals in front of the TV were common fare. Two doors on one side presumably led to bedrooms. At the rear was the smallest kitchen I had ever seen. A table, littered with papers, filled an area intended for dining. The door to the bathroom was ajar.

"Do you think it too cold to sit on the balcony, Mr. Taber?"

"Not at all."

We sat in uncomfortable plastic chairs with a table between us.

LOST RIVER BRIDGE

Fifteen minutes passed while we talked about my immediate family and hers. I saw no evidence of discomfort. Her talk was genial and bright. In a few moments, she popped up and asked if I would like a drink. I didn't think she meant alcohol, and we agreed on my preference for hot tea. Presently, she returned with a tea tray and three cups. An obese young woman in her late twenties followed her.

"This is my daughter, Rachel."

Rachel put a large plate of cookies on the table without offering me one. She greeted me with a hug and said, "I understand we're related."

"I believe that's true, but I cannot define the path."

"Who cares! We never see any of the family anyway. Mother and I are, well, what would you call it, ostracized?" In my surprise, I suppose I looked up rather quickly. "Maybe that's too strong a word," she added before I spoke. "Discarded might be more accurate."

"Really! I'm surprised. Do you feel the same way, Annie?"

Annie took a deep breath. "Do you take anything in your tea?" I noted Rachel was already on her second cookie.

"Just a touch of sugar, if you would, please." She passed the cup. I nodded my thanks and said nothing, waiting for Annie to answer my question. Clearly, she had not forgotten, and I imagined she debated her choices. When she spoke, I was even more surprised. Her voice was bitter.

"It's that husband of Irene's who makes all the trouble."

"Emery! Emery makes trouble for you! What do you mean?"

A torrent of hate mixed with alleged abuse poured out. She did not whine, suggest self-incrimination, or hint that she shared the blame. I heard only hostility. It was a strange story.

"When I was little, the church held a fund-raising fair. Mother said I was to go with Irene, but when I went to the outhouse, Emery locked me in."

The abruptness of her statement astonished me. I managed to veil my reaction although it was on the tip of my tongue to challenge her. She continued without a pause, plainly unaware of my reaction. I resolved to listen to her story with unbiased objectivity.

"Then he and Irene ran away somewhere. They didn't go to the fair because nobody saw either one of them. The next day, Irene whined and whimpered until Mother couldn't stand it any more. Sunday night Irene told Mother she did it. But, I know she lied to protect Emery. Ever since she was a little kid, she's loved Emery. She used to boast about it and tell me someday she'd marry him. It was spiteful the way she did it, like she meant nobody would ever marry me.

"She and Emery didn't even come to my wedding. When I asked her why, she said it was because I made a mistake and Jimmy was a drunken no-good. Then, when I got a divorce, she gloated and said stuff like, 'I told you so,' and all that.

"She's always writing soupy letters like she thinks we should get together to settle our problem. She goes to Timmy and he writes to me and says to see Irene and stop the foolishness. Well, it's not foolishness. It's meanness, that's what it is. And not on my part.

"But, I know what she wants. She wants the letter back. She doesn't care about my daughter or me. I won't go to see her because she'll whine and whimper all syrupy-like until she gets it. It's him puts her up to all this stuff. She doesn't care about the letter. She just wants it because I have it. Oh! I hate that man."

I held my tongue despite her tirade. I wanted to interrupt several times. By not speaking, however, I had the opportunity to think about ways of reconciling the sisters. Should I or should I not tell her about my close friendship with Emery and Irene? I decided to tell her then and there because she would accuse me of deception if she learned the facts later. She took the information well.

"I've heard the story about locking you in the outhouse. The version I heard is different, but you could resolve that by meeting with Irene. If I have learned anything about Lost River Bridge, it's that the same story told by two different people seldom comes out the same way. But, Annie, there is more to this conflict than who did or did not lock you in the outhouse. You speak of a letter. Would you care to tell me about it?" I presumed Irene or Emery had written an unintentional comment that Annie distorted as proof of their contempt. Surely, the missing letter taken from the family Bible could not be the issue. Gracious! They were only children. But still, maybe it could.

Annie looked at her daughter who had consumed half the cookies. Their eyes locked and I saw a silent question between a mother and a daughter who loved each other. Rachel gave a subtle shake of her head, almost unnoticeable.

"I think not," Annie said.

"Very well," I said. "It is not my business to pry into your personal affairs. I would like to be a goodwill ambassador. With your permission, may I tell Irene and Emery how you feel about them?"

The answer was instantaneous, strong, and defiant. "No!"

I shrugged and looked away. "That tells me, then, that you do not want to defend your version of the incident."

"Why should I?"

"Because life is too short to harbor such hostility." I had no idea if my plea made any impression, but I wanted to continue the conversation until I learned the nature of the letter that I now knew was the root of the problem. Her intensity suggested a cool-down period would help. "Would you pour me another cup of tea, please?"

She froze for an instant. I felt sure she toyed with the idea of refusing and asking me to leave. My outstretched hand held the teacup and saucer. For whatever reason, she seemed to concede defeat, took the cup, poured and passed it back, forgetting the sugar.

"Thank you." I smiled as I watched her fill her own cup. We bantered awhile about generalities. At a lull in the conversation, I tossed out what I hoped would be an innocent statement. "By the way, you didn't tell me what letter you referred to."

Again, her shifting eyes made a quizzical look at Rachel, who came in on cue. "Might I have another cup, please mother?"

"Oh! I'm sorry, dear. Of course."

Annie filled her daughter's cup, topped her own cup and stirred in milk and sugar, which she had done only a few moments before.

"Wh ... wh ... what business are you in, Elijah?"

"I'm retired. I was in the building business. Paper mills in Canada mostly."

She sipped her tea. I did likewise in the pause that followed. Then the three of us took a second sip simultaneously.

"Did you enjoy that kind of work?"

"Very much."

Again, we sipped in silence. I saw a tinge of color rising in Annie's cheeks. I guessed Rachel did, too, because she mumbled about homework for tomorrow's lesson and excused herself. She entered the apartment and returned immediately.

"Mother, would you show me where you put your workbook, please?" It was clumsy, but I gave her marks for trying.

Annie turned to look at Rachel standing in the doorway. Then, she floored me.

"Rachel, please get the letter from the strong box."

"No, Moth—"

"Rachel! Get the letter!"

"Yes, Mother."

Annie and I sat in silence. Rachel returned. She handed an envelope to her mother and left shaking her head. Annie stood with it in her hand, waving it in my face.

"Mr. Taber! You came here today under a pretense. You don't care a hoot about Irene, Emery or me. You came to get this letter. I don't know why and I don't care why." I rose to protest, but she continued without a pause. "You see, Mr. Taber, I have the letter. I took it out of the family Bible on the day they locked me in the outhouse. I admit, I took it for spite because I couldn't even read at the time. Later, nobody asked about the letter. In all the years since, nobody has ever asked except Irene. I know Mother didn't care. How could she care? She had three little children to look after when her husband went to war. Almost before she knew it, he was dead. Left alone to provide for her family, she never even thought about the letter. I have had it since I was four. And you, Mr. Taber, will never read it. I'll thank you to leave now."

Episode Sixteen

Something Did Happen

The bickering between Irene and Annie was none of my business. After wavering for a few days, I decided I should apologize and telephoned Emery for advice.

"That's right," he said. "You poked your nose in where it didn't belong." I wanted to interject that forty-two years had passed since I last heard such stern displeasure in his voice, but I checked the impulse. "The best idea for you is butt out. Irene and Annie have squabbled for years. There's no telling who's at fault, but I'm sorry to say that Annie distorts the events. She's harbored her grievance so long it's become irrefutable in her mind. We pray her heart will soften, but whatever your purpose, Elijah, you can't change anything."

I accepted his reproof and was about to ask his recommendation as to how I should go about apologizing, when he said, "Maybe you'd like to know about … ." The surprise of his abrupt stop left me tongue-tied. "Oh! Never mind," he added as if he realized the futility of more explanation. "You wouldn't understand."

"Emery, I don't know what's on your mind, but if it's a private family matter, you're right, I wouldn't understand. More than that, I don't want to know. I only want to apologize for my intrusion."

"Well … ." He drew the word out, and I suspected he yearned to tell me a story. Typical Emery, he had not changed. Whatever notion gnawed inside him screamed to escape.

"Go ahead," I said. "Tell me what's on your mind."

I never expect the unusual in normal conversations. With my mind on Irene and Annie, I forgot that talking with Emery is not normal. In his low, secretive voice, his extrasensory experiences always came as a surprise.

"I saw Granny Sarah last Saturday night."

Seated at my desk with the phone cradled on my shoulder, I stifled my laugh and managed a cough instead. "Excuse me. Must be something in my throat. Did you say Granny Sarah?"

"Yes."

"Are you sure?"

"Of course, I'm sure. You don't believe me."

"Sure I do. It's just that you took me by surprise. Tell me what happened."

"Nothing."

"Emery! Granny died a hundred and fifty years ago. You saw her on Saturday night, and you say nothing happened. Something must have happened."

"I know when she died," he replied as if insulted. I forgot seeing Granny Sarah was an ordinary event for him.

"Tell me about it," I stammered, fearing perhaps my protests might discourage him. They didn't. He was bursting to tell me.

"We had our monthly potluck supper at the church Saturday night. Lots of people come for storytelling. Too bad you wasn't with us; there was some funny stories."

Emery had done a commendable job over the years, promoting himself from country boy to local pastor. He worked hard for several years of dedicated correspondence school to achieve his goal. But, when it came to storytelling, he slipped back to the ungrammatical voice of the Ozark yarn spinner.

"The one I liked best," he continued, "was 'bout them pastors having trouble with armadillos chewing up the lawns in front of the churches. No matter what they done, the pastors couldn't drive those varmints away. One fellow set cages and trapped them. He took them way out in the country and let them go. Soon as he freed them, the varmints started running. They run so fast, they beat him back to his church. The second fellow tried poison. The varmints loved it. They invited their friends; the pastor had more varmints than ever on his grass. The third fellow had no trouble getting rid of his. He called them together and said if they was going to mess up his grass, they'd have to help support the church for the cost of maintaining the lawn. Then he gave them envelopes, and he ain't seen a varmint since."

"I'm sorry I wasn't there to hear such great tales, but I want to hear what happened with Granny Sarah."

"I told you, nothing happened. I cleaned up a bit after the party. 'Bout half past ten, I started home. The sky was black, no moon, or stars, or nothing. It wasn't stormy, or anything like that. A wind blew through the trees; nothing special except for the darkness. Irene went home early. I walked along thinking about the evening. I didn't eat much; I've been having indigestion lately. I don't know what it is, but I'm off my food. Pastor Grimes from Gainesville had a good tale. He told us about—"

I feared I was in for an ear-bending night of stories. "I don't want to hear about the church supper, or any funny pastor jokes. I want to know what happened about Granny."

The telephone was silent. Oh, Lord, I thought, I've hurt his feelings. "Hello! Hello! Emery! You still there?"

"Yeah. Yeah. I'm here," he mumbled. "Where was I?"

"You were walking home in the dark after supper."

"I 'member. That's right. It was real dark. I didn't bring no flashlight. Shucks! I don't need one. I've been walking that road for forty years. Know every stone and every bend. Passing the cemetery—you know, one foot on the grass, one foot on the gravel so I'd keep my bearings—I heard a noise.

"'Emmmmeeeeerrrryyy'.

"I stopped dead still to listen. Aw shucks! I figured it was a bird or maybe the wind in the trees. I started walking again when that strange sound come again.

"'Emmmmeeeeerrrryyy'.

"Someone called me. I couldn't believe it. I stopped and shouted, 'Who is it?'

"A faint voice come from a long ways off. Ever so faint, I heard it again. 'It's Granny Sarah.' It sounded so faint, I didn't think she was in the cemetery like she usually was. I worried about maybe she wasn't there at all, lost, or couldn't find her way home, or something.

"'Where are you, Granny?'

"'Over here,' she squeaked. 'Over here, in the corner of the cemetery.'

"'What do you want, Granny?'

"'I want to talk to somebody. It's lonely back here.'

Emery told the story well, modulating his voice between the squeaky sound of Granny, and the usual deep tones for himself.

"Well," he continued, "I started into the cemetery looking for the corner she was in. I figured she'd be in the southwest corner near her grave so I started in that direction. Like I said, it was pitch-black, and I couldn't see anything. I felt my way past the stones, but I clean forgot about the new Gregory Treadwell stone. You remember him, Elijah? He was the sneaky boy who come to the cemetery that summer you was here. You used to tell him to go to the lake, and if he didn't go he'd have to work. I remember one time you went after little Greg and—"

"Emery, don't start another story. Just tell me about Granny Sarah. You were in the cemetery, and then what happened?"

"Nothing," he said.

"Something must have happened. What did you do?"

"I tripped over the stone, that's what I did. It's a small one, eighteen or twenty inches tall. I tripped over that stone and cut my shin. I reached down to feel my leg, and it was wet with blood. I mean, it streamed down my leg. I figured I cut right into a blood vessel. I could feel it running down my leg. I took out my handkerchief and tied it right tight to stop the bleeding. After I got done doing the bandage, I limped through the cemetery with my eyes watering from the pain; I couldn't see anything. I yelled again.

"'Where are you, Granny?'

"'Over here,' she squeaked. 'Over here, in the corner of the cemetery.'

"When I heard her this time I realized I was going the wrong way. She was in the southeast corner and I'd gone the other way, to the southwest.

LOST RIVER BRIDGE

"'Just a minute, Granny,' I shouted, 'I'll be right there.'

"When I turned I saw a light shining through the trees. I couldn't make out what it was. It wasn't a lantern. It wasn't a star. I couldn't tell what it was. It was just a light shining through the trees."

"For Heaven's sake, Emery," I said, "tell me what happened."

"Nothing," he said.

"Nothing? What do you mean nothing Was she there?"

"'Course she was. I didn't see her at first. I limped towards the light with my leg throbbing terrible-like when I seen something. The light was like a huge Chinese lantern spilling a faint glow over the ground. You couldn't hardly believe it, Elijah, but I seen a blanket with the finest picnic spread you'd ever want to see. Wow! What a spread! Sliced ham and fried chicken, baked beans with homemade rolls, cookies and cake, and lemonade all setting there on the blanket. There was even ants crawling over it. Until that moment, I wasn't hungry. Like I said, I didn't eat at the church supper, but suddenly, I was hungry. First time I felt like eating in weeks. I was glad I didn't eat at the church supper. I was mighty hungry and couldn't take my eyes off the food.

"Then I seen her. She was setting in a rocking chair, like in the picture in the Fireside Café. You remember that picture used to hang in the old meeting hall that summer you was here? You remember that, Elijah?"

"Emery! I remember the picture, but that doesn't matter, and don't start another story. Just tell me what happened?"

"Nothing happened. I told you that before."

"Did you talk to her?"

"'Course I did. We had a nice talk. Frieda is well, but the two of them is still worried about Granny's medallion. Sometimes she gets awful cross when she thinks about it. I keep telling her it ain't my fault, but she won't listen. She thinks it's up to me to find it. And I say, how am I going to find it? She says she doesn't know; ask Elijah, she says."

"Me?"

"No! She means Elijah Pursey."

"I hope so," I said, somewhat disturbed feeling that Granny had assigned me a responsibility I didn't want. "What happened about the food?"

"We ate most of it." This was too much. It's one thing to see ghosts and have them assign tasks for the living, but to see them eat was ridiculous.

"She ate something?"

"Well," he hesitated and then he confessed. "Truth is she didn't eat much. I ate most of it, if I have to tell the truth."

"What did she eat?"

"She ate a ham sandwich. I know that 'cause I could see it in her insides."

"You what? You could see it?"

"'Course I could see it. She was setting in the chair, I could see right through her. I could see the whole chair right through her. It was the same chair like in the picture. I could see the sandwich in her insides, too. It was right there, the whole thing."

By this time, I was ready to fight back a little. I figured he was deep enough into his story that he wouldn't quit. He was having too much fun, and the tale was too good not to finish.

"Now listen to me, Emery. I've asked you about ten times, what happened, and every time you say nothing. What do you mean nothing happened? First, you saw Granny Sarah, and you say nothing happened. In the middle of the night, you saw her, and all you can say is nothing happened! Then you saw her eating! What's the matter with you, Emery?"

"Ain't nothing the matter with me," he said. "What's the matter with you, Elijah? You afeared of ghosts, are you?"

I avoided laughing. "Emery, I don't understand how you can say nothing happened. You saw a real live ghost of Granny Sarah! You saw her eat a ham sandwich! And you keep saying nothing happened."

I waited for a response, but nothing came. Maybe I went too far, and my tirade upset him. I was about to apologize when he spoke in a soft quiet voice like a choirboy at confession.

"Well, to tell the truth", he said, "something did happen. When

LOST RIVER BRIDGE

the party was over, Granny said she was tired and wanted to get some rest. Soon as she said that everything kind of, well, sort of faded away. The light in the tree grew dim. There was enough for me to see my way to the gate without tripping over any more stones. When I got there, I looked back to watch the light grow dimmer until it went out.

"You 'member how I told you I cut my leg terrible when I fell over the Treadwell stone, and how I tied my handkerchief around it to stop the bleeding."

"I haven't forgotten."

"When I got home, I went to the kitchen sink to clean up and wash the blood away thinking maybe I'd have to go to the hospital for stitches. Well, I just can't explain it, Elijah. I rolled up my pant leg to look; there wasn't nothing there. No cut, no blood, no nothing. I looked at my handkerchief, and it didn't have one drop of blood on it. So you're right Elijah, something did happen, and I plumb forgot all about it till this minute. Yes sir, really was something."

I could hear his breathing in the long pause that followed. Then he spoke in a voice filled with awe as if he had witnessed a miracle.

"How would you explain that, Elijah?"

"Emery, I couldn't possibly explain it, but I'd like to ask you a question."

"What's that?"

"When you woke up in the morning, were you hungry?"

He didn't answer. About five seconds later, I heard a faint click. The line went dead, and I hung up.

Afterwards, I realized he avoided advising me how to apologize to Annie and Irene. I guessed I'd have to figure it out alone.

The next morning, I lay in bed, stared at the ceiling, and wondered if his devious mind offered the subtle suggestion that he really wanted me to pursue the trail of the medal.

Episode Seventeen

A True Story

I bought land and began to design my dream home, free from the restraints of earning a living. After almost half a century of toil responding to the dictates of time and money, I delighted in answering only to myself. I managed to match my resources to a unique design that avoided the sterile quality of low-cost homes.

Irene called two weeks before Christmas to announce a shopping spree in northwest Arkansas.

"Let me drive you down. I know where we can stay in a comfortable Bed and Breakfast for a few days."

"I was only going for a day. I hadn't planned on staying overnight. You know how Emery is. He's—"

"Don't be silly. Bundle him up, and I'll pick you up in the morning. It would be an honor for me to escort him around town."

When I arrived, Emery's appearance shocked me. Irene was her usual self, but he looked pallid, moving with a graceless lethargy. We stayed four nights, the first two marred by Emery's lassitude. On the third day, he perked up a little, and we did a mini-tour of downtown Fayetteville while Irene engaged in the female diversion called shopping.

"Have you traveled much, Emery?"

"No. And I don't want to."

"I suppose you've been to Kansas City and St Louis."

"Never. I've always been happy in my own backyard with my garden and church. Nothing in this world could possibly equal them."

My means of judging his comfort level was the frequency of his stories, which came to life that afternoon. I guessed he'd told them a thousand times or more, but they were new to me. Lazy afternoons seemed to be his favorite time. Storytelling restored his air of confidence as it did in the old days when we loitered in the cemetery.

"The Catholic Church yonder makes me think of Father Joe Lalonde," he said as we strolled along Lafayette Street. "He was involved in the memorial business at the bridge. Great sense of humor, I'll tell you that. He'd call once in awhile to ask for a story he could tell on Sunday morning. I'd dream up something, and he'd laugh his head off. I doubt he ever used my yarns in church, but who knows, maybe he did."

We walked on in silence, the usual quiet moment before a story. He motioned towards a bench, and we sat in the sunshine. On a beautiful December afternoon, this was the tale from the Catholic Church.

"Joe wasn't such a bad storyteller for a fellow not born to it. One time he told me 'bout a celebration happened on a Saturday afternoon in his parish hall. As I remember, it was the fortieth wedding anniversary of Ashley and Lillian somebody. Their last name don't matter; I'll call them Jones.

"Father had his sleeves rolled up at work in the rectory when the doorbell rang. When Joe opened the door, an old man smiled at him. The visitor wore a white dress shirt, a black string tie, red suspenders, and a dirty gray fedora,

"'Excuse me,' said the old fellow. 'There ain't nobody in the office, and the door's locked. I banged a few times, but I didn't get no answer.'

"Joe asked what he wanted. The fellow said he needed a room for the night. This baffled Father. I mean, the old man was well dressed even if a little out of the ordinary. But he didn't look destitute like the sort that usually asked for lodging in the rectory.

"'Well, it's this away,' said the man. 'I got this here invite to a party on account of a wedding that's going on. It come in the mail 'bout a week ago. It said a Mr. Jones was getting married here today. I guess I must have met him one time, else I don't understand why an invite was sent to me if it ain't him. Since somebody went to the trouble of sending it, I thought the least I could do was show up. I didn't know where I was going until I come around the bend in the road. I seen this here Bed and Breakfast place you run. Your business must be good since you ain't got nobody working the office this time of day.'

"Father didn't know if this old bird was serious or part of the act. He decided he'd play along to see what happened. 'Yes,' Joe said, 'business is good. I'm doing all right even with the office locked up.'

"'Ain't that something,' said the old man. 'I knowed a lot of motel owners who'd like to learn how you done it.'

"'Who are you?'

"The old fellow smiled and took a long time to answer, 'A lost soul,' he said with a big smile on his face.

"When he said that, Father figured for sure this guy was playing a trick. 'In that case you come to the right place,' Joe said, 'and you better come on in.'

"They talked a bit. The old fellow claimed he didn't know anything 'bout the Catholic Church. Joe took him on a tour through the sanctuary. Moving down the aisle, he said, 'The stations are over here.'

"'Stations! You got stations here? Where's the tracks?'"

Emery began to laugh. "That became a joke between Joe and me. He'd call and say, 'This is the station manager speaking. I'm looking for somebody to man the switches.' Or sometimes he'd say, 'Ride the caboose or shovel coal.' It was dumb and it ain't funny when you tell it. After you toss it back and forth a few times, it gets to be a private joke that you laugh at every time you hear it, even though you've heard it a hundred times before. It gets funnier as time goes by. I think kids today call it corny."

Emery was quiet for a few moments. I imagined his thoughts dwelled on Joe Lalonde who died ten or twelve years before. With a little start, he freed himself from his reverie and went on with the tale.

"Anyway, Joe asked his visitor to kneel at the altar steps, and he said a blessing for him. The old boy thought that was wonderful; first time in his life, so he said, anybody ever prayed for him. Afterwards, he told Joe he feared someone up there in charge of answering prayers was going to yell down, "WHO?"

"'Course, by this time, if the fellow didn't know before, he knew now Joe was the parish priest, but he didn't let on. He asked where Mr. Jones was going to be married.

"'That's Ash and Lil,' Father said.

"'Nope,' says the old man. 'The name on my invite says Jones.'

"'Yes,' Joe said, 'Ash and Lil. They're celebrating their marriage today with their children and grandchildren.'

"'Can't be,' the old man replied. 'I don't know nobody named Ashenlil. I'm certain the name I seen on the invite was Jones. If he's just getting married today, he can't have a whole bunch of kids and grandkids. Besides, if it were Ashenlil, I wouldn't have received an invite since I don't know nobody named Ashenlil.'

"The old man put his hand on Father's arm and thought about what he said. 'What if I'm wrong? You think maybe we ought to say another prayer for this Jones fellow in case we're mixed up or something.'

"Father scratched his head and looked worried while he pondered the question. Then he said he didn't think it necessary. If Jones fathered all those children and wasn't married, it was too late, and if they were wrong, it didn't matter anyway.

"The old fellow had no idea what Joe meant, and of course, Joe didn't either. The visitor didn't ask for an explanation. Instead, he inquired where the celebration would take place. Father led him down the stairs to the parish hall. The old man didn't recognize a soul. As bold as a strutting peacock, he walked to the front of the room and asked if there was anybody present by the name of Ashenlil. If so, would they please step forward?

"Mr. Jones came to the front accompanied by a woman. The old fellow greeted them. 'Mr. and Mrs. Ashenlil, it's sure a pleasure to meet you. Your friend, Joe, that fellow standing by the window, he sent me here. I tell you he's a right nice fellow. Come up here, Joe.' Father stepped forward, and the old man put his arm around his shoulder. 'What's your last name, Joe? Oh! Joe's your last name. First name is Father! Father Joe! That's a real nice name. Shake hands with Mr. and Mrs. Ashenlil, Father.'

"Soon as they shook, he dragged Father off to the side out of earshot. He whispered in Joe's ear. 'We got a real problem here,' he said. 'Them two over there, the two you just shook hands with, them ain't Mr. and Mrs. Ashenlil. That's Mr. Jones. He's the one with kids and grandkids, and he's getting married to day! Father, I've seen him before. No mistake! No mistake at all. Maybe you and I better go back to the church and start praying. Maybe we better go quick, Father, and see if you can save a transgressor. Come on, Father, hurry.'"

The story stopped so abruptly, I asked, "Is that the end?"

"Yep."

"Did they ever find out who the guy was?"

"Don't know. Joe never said."

The evening before we returned home, the three of us enjoyed a pre-Christmas dinner catered by our hosts at the B&B. Emery trotted out his collection of anecdotes, including a tale about Bessie Taber and the Lost River Emporium that took place about 1900.

"Bessie always managed to be about a hundred years behind the times. She decided to leap into the twentieth century with what was then brand new office equipment; a mechanical tabulating machine for accounting and a typewriter, if you can believe it.

"There wasn't a soul in Lost River Bridge knew how to calculate or type. In Springfield, where she bought the equipment, she went to the newspaper office to place a help-wanted ad. The ad-man asked all kinds of questions that Bessie didn't rightly understand. When he asked if the applicant needed to be bilingual, Bessie thought that was great idea as how a few French-speaking folks lived in the area.

"A few weeks after the ad appeared, a dog entered the store. He jumped on the chair, rolled a sheet of paper into the typewriter, typed for a few moments, withdrew an application for the job, and presented it to Bessie.

"This floored her. When she recovered, she shook her head. Despite the accuracy of the perfect letter, Bessie said, 'I can't hire you, I need somebody who can operate this here calculator.'

"She watched in awe as the animal pawed the keys, pulled the lever, punched and pulled again, and showed her the answer to a complex mathematical problem.

"'You sure are a smart dog,' Bessie said. The animal wagged its tail and wiggled around. 'Woof, woof,' it barked ready to start work right away.

"'Wait a minute,' Bessie said, 'I can't offer you no job. I want a bilingual employee.'

"The dog sat, turned its head to one side and said, 'Meow.'

"Everybody in Lost River Bridge trooped in to the Emporium to see the dog at work. It was a great sensation. I saw that dog with my own eyes. Cleverest animal I ever saw. I don't know if you've noticed how dogs hang around the Emporium now-a-days. That's 'cause after that dog died, there's been an opening for a new employee but there ain't one of them can speak French."

Over coffee, Emery talked about the river flowing in two directions. I had not forgotten the tale of the tanker fish but I wouldn't spoil his storytelling with something as mundane as the truth.

"Yes sir," he said, "when I was a boy, professors from the universities come to Lost River Bridge to investigate how it was the river flowed in two directions at the same time. I remember a fellow from Rolla. I took him up to the headwaters. We had our camping gear, food, and so on. After we lit the campfire, he produced a bottle of whiskey. Now, I'm not a drinker, never have been, but he persuaded me to take a nip, which I did a couple of times. I can't remember if we ate supper, or what we did. The next thing I knew, I woke up under a starry sky. I saw the professor was awake, so we commenced to talk.

"'Professor, look up at the sky and tell me what you see,' I said.

"'I see a beautiful sky and thousands of stars.'

"'Does that suggest anything?' I asked.

STEPHEN P. BYERS

"In a few moments, he said, 'On one of those stars millions of miles away lies a camper staring upward and wondering if somewhere in the universe another creature is doing the same. Emery, you and I are the other creatures. If I took my flashlight, I could send a message into space that would someday arrive on his planet.'

"'Wonderful,' I said. 'And what would you say?'

"'I don't know. Do you have something to suggest?'

"'I think you should ask if he forgot to put his tent up, too.'"

I guess Irene was Emery's conscience. This time she said, "I never knew you to take a drink." Emery's blush colored his face making him look better than I had seen since his arrival. He stared at her as the room fell silent. I feared for a dreadful moment he was about to chastise her. I was wrong. He was too gentle for that.

"Irene," he said, "in the experiences of life, you never grasp the essential element of what's going on around you. You see, my dear, you must always take advantage of the opportunity to tell a good tale by putting the story ahead of the truth."

She smiled. It did my heart good to see two people so genuinely in love after a lifetime together.

"I'll tell you a story," she said, "a happy story that's the absolute truth. Today, I went to see Annie. There was no one home when I arrived so I sat on the doorstep and waited. Rachel came home first. She was surprised, but not as surprised as Annie when she came in. Rachel and I drank tea while we waited. She was cordial but a little shy. Annie, on the other hand, was aggressive. We talked for most of an hour. I did nearly all the talking about home, about Mother, about our life together, and growing up with Timothy. I told her those memories were too dear to cast aside because of a silly childhood incident. She challenged me, but when she finished, to my great surprise, Rachel took control. She looked at Annie and said, 'Mother, I don't understand. This is your sister. I wish I had a sister.' Then Rachel came to me and gave me a hug. I thanked her, and said to Annie, 'Please, think about us,' and I left."

"Gee, Irene," I said, "the greatest gift you could get for your Christmas would be a softening of Annie's heart."

Episode Eighteen

The Mallow Birds

The warm temperatures and light rain in February encouraged the spring growth. Daffodils, forsythia, quince, and dogwood blossoms colored the gardens two or three weeks ahead of schedule. In Lost River Bridge, on the first weekend of March, Emery's garden was not quite in full bloom, but bright with color just the same. The temperature dropped all day Monday bringing snow in the afternoon. I ate supper with Irene and Emery. When it came time to leave, the intensity of the snow had increased. They persuaded me I should stay the night. Tuesday morning ten inches of wet snow buried everything.

Emery canceled his fishing trip with somebody named Pete who I never met. "I'm not going to shovel the walk, Pete," he said into the telephone, "and that's final." He replaced the receiver and switched off the weather channel. "Won't be any cars come down the road till the snow melts in four or five days." He sulked at the kitchen table ignoring Irene doing the breakfast dishes.

"Now, Emery Taber, you go do your job like a good boy." Irene turned from the sink and smiled at him, her hands on her hips, suds dripping to the floor. Their eyes met for an instant before he seized his coffee mug and lowered his head. "You know the snow may not be gone by Sunday. It's up to you to clear the paths." She turned back to her chores.

"Did you hear me?"

"Yeah. I heard."

Emery dragged himself to his feet. "Come on," he said. He handed me a shovel from the porch as we went out. We cleared a path to the road. He leaned on the fence and sighed. The door slammed and a moment later Irene's voice descended on us.

"Pete called. He didn't know if he could get the tractor out but he's going to meet you at the church, one way or the other."

It wasn't like Emery to be upset with Irene. I wondered about his health as he glanced over his shoulder and left her standing on the porch, her apron flapping in the breeze. The snow hindered our pace. Twice, I lost my balance, but managed to recover both times without falling. We cleared the entrance walk to the church. The exercise did nothing to improve his mood. Pete never arrived, which made his tantrum worse.

"Let's go to the Fireside café for coffee," he said.

Most of the regulars were there, hunched over their morning coffee, muttering about the weather. A fellow I didn't know sauntered in. His weather-beaten face broke into a broad grin. For the first time that day, Emery brightened up.

"Well, if ain't the great politician in the flesh. Elijah Taber meet Bill Hawkins. If there's anybody in Ozark County who can explain everything there is to know, it's Bill Hawkins. What about this global warming stuff, Bill? How come we're getting snow when the world's supposed to be getting hotter?"

"Ain't nothing but a little mix-up," he said.

With the eye of an expert sharpshooter, he flipped his hat on to the shelf above the coat rack. He struggled out of his jacket and settled on to a stool. Eloise had his coffee poured and on the counter before Bill took his seat. He lit a cigarette exhaling with audible satisfaction.

Emery whispered in my ear. "Watch this. After years of campaigning and seven successful elections, he knows how to work the crowd."

Bill brushed off the clamoring demand for an explanation with a casual wave of his hand. "Them scientific fellows," he said, "done hung their thermometers upside down."

Eloise seemed to force a smile while everybody else guffawed. Bill didn't miss a beat. "Puts me in mind of the year we had the big snow in October. Remember that, boys?"

LOST RIVER BRIDGE

As near as anyone could tell afterwards the opinions were unanimous; no one present had ever seen snow in October, but somebody remembered a story about Abner Applehorn saying there'd been a frosty day in July once.

"I 'member it clearly," said Bill. "Surely y'all 'member that couple come here wanting to take pictures of the Mallow birds."

It didn't sound funny to me, but it brought a round of laughter and slapping of knees that nearly shook the building amid a chorus of demands that Bill tell the story again.

"Yes, sir," he said, "that was a cold October morning. We was setting right here in the café when the door opened. A man and woman come in; good-looking couple, mid-thirties perhaps, no older. Wearing bright red, fur-lined jackets, they were; camouflage pants and heavy boots; red hunting caps with corduroy earflaps tied over the top. Yes, sir! They was dressed for the wilderness, all right.

"'Hell-ooo,' the man said, like he was in the Alps or some yodeling place. 'My name is Tommy. This here is my wife Martha.'

"'Sit down over there,' Eloise said. 'Coffee?'

"'No thanks, we're looking for directions.'

"'Where to?'

"'We're free-lance photographers on assignment. We want to get pictures of the Mallow birds.'

"Boom! Conversation stopped just like that. You could hear the mice scratching in the cellar. Everybody stared at them. Then one by one, the faces turned away, hands covering their smiles. I'm pretty sure Andy spoke up first. 'Ain't been no sightings for some time now,' he said. 'What you got in mind?'

"'We need to know the best place to search for them.'

"Andy toyed with his coffee, his back to the strangers so they couldn't see his grin. 'Well now,' he said, 'far as we know, the last sighting was up the mountains. What kind of vehicle you driving?'

"'Four-wheel-drive truck. Goes through snow like nothing.'

"'You're going to need it, if you're going after Mallow birds.'

"He gave them directions and the weather discussion resumed as if them visitors didn't exist.

"Eloise asked, 'Could I get you a sandwich or something?'

"'No, thanks,' Tommy said. 'We had a good breakfast and we're anxious to get going.'

"Andy swiveled off his stool to watch the Land Rover pass the Emporium, turn up the hill and disappear around the bend. 'Dang fools,' he said into his empty cup."

"I know you're all going to laugh," I said, "but what is a Mallow bird?"

"Eloise, pour me a coffee," Bill said, "while I educate Elijah."

"When Lucien Bellechase had his still back in the woods, he humped his supplies in fifty-pound sacks. One day as he trudged along the streambed, a huge bird attacked him. Being unprepared for such an event, he dropped his load and dove for cover. You know a big bird can scare you bad. Lucien said he'd never seen the likes of it. 'Big as an albatross,' he said, although the truth was he'd never seen an albatross.

"Well, sir, that there bird ripped into them burlap bags and ate about ten pounds of grain before he could chase him off. 'Course, the question was where did a bird like that come from and how was it he'd never seen one before? He got to scouting about and found five or six of them down to the North Fork of the White River. Near as he could figure, them birds had been flying north with the geese, but quit on account of they was either too big or too lazy to maintain the pace. Lost and bewildered, not knowing where they was, and having trouble finding feed, seemed like the humane thing to do was dispose of them birds and be done with it.

"Lucien was about to shoot them when he had an idea. He figured if he could lure them to the still, they'd be perfect for scaring off the revenuers. It took a little while but he succeeded by setting out grain. Ever week or so, he moved the feed a half-mile towards the still, and left a trail of grain for the birds to follow. By the end of summer, those birds fattened up and begun to enjoy life.

"Lucien noticed when he cleaned the tanks, the birds hustled round back of the still to sample the wastewater. Naturally, the discharge had a little alcohol left in it. That made Lucien kind of curious, so he rigged up a trough and poured in some moonshine.

"Them birds took to drinking pretty heavy. They'd howl and carouse until three or four in the morning. Their squawk was somewhere between the hoot of an owl, and the bray of a donkey. If a stranger came by, no matter what time of day or night, they'd attack because they were either drunk, and didn't know what they were doing, or hung over and didn't want to be woke up. They was better than watchdogs at spotting revenuers.

"There come a time when Lucien tried to ease the birds off the booze by handing out fishing poles and teaching them to cast for bass in the river. They didn't like fishing, but they sure liked them poles. They'd walk around flailing at one another as they fought over the moonshine. The poles turned out to be pretty good weapons for scaring off revenuers, too.

"Folks didn't know what them birds were called so they gave them the name Mallow birds, not because they spent most of their time in a mellow mood, but because they was colored like roasted marshmallows.

"To the best of anybody's knowledge, Mallow birds are extinct now. The government considered it a bad example to put them on the endangered species list 'cause of their addiction to alcohol."

I loved these people and their stories. As I looked around the quiet room, I saw men nodding their heads and drinking in the story, deadly serious like they'd never heard the tale before.

"Go on with your story, Bill," Andy said.

"Well, it was like this. After they left the Fireside Café, Tommy and Martha took the old road out of town; the one that goes past the

Schumacher house that burned years ago. The fire destroyed the back of the house. The front wall never collapsed. It's still there. A piece of the roof hung from the chimney making a shelter where the ghost was said to live. Every Halloween, kids visited the house to hear the ghost of Herman Schumacher snarl and screech. No one ever sighted it, but folks say it shrieks like a Mallow bird.

"They got to the top of the mountain after lunch and set out on their search. The weather turned bad in the afternoon. Dark clouds come racing across the sky. When the front passed, the temperature dropped, bringing snow and freezing rain.

"'We better get out of here,' Tommy said. 'There's not a soul knows where we are. If the roads wash out, we could be in trouble.'

"They loaded the truck in the fading daylight. The twisting mountain road to Lost River Bridge was mighty hard to follow. The sleet blinded them and iced the windshield as they curled down the mountain trail. The truck lurched from side to side in the ruts. Suddenly, it veered sideways and plunged downwards. It come to a stop face first in a deep ravine. And wouldn't you know it, both headlights smashed. There they was, shivering in the darkness, alone in an ice storm without no idea where they was.

"You and me, we might have panicked, but not Tommy and Martha. No sir, they knew how to survive in the wilderness. They was prepared for any emergency. Sometimes, the best laid plans; well, y'all know how it is. There come a series of events what left them in a hopeless mess. The left front tire went flat. The spare, mounted between the headlights, was wedged in the ditch. Tommy fixed the winch to pull the truck on to the road. Just as the winch took the full load, the cable ratchet broke. Tommy lost his footing, tumbled backwards and kicked the toolbox over the edge. He watched the emergency light, which he had set on the box, bouncing down until it come to rest a hundred feet or more below. It flickered for a moment and went out. The worst of it was, their flashlights was packed in the toolbox. Stuck in the dark, the sleet pelting them, they didn't have no hope of freeing the truck.

"'It's only a mile or two to the village,' Tommy said. 'Let's start walking.'

LOST RIVER BRIDGE

"Tommy didn't figure right. Maybe he said it so Martha wouldn't be too scared. They slithered and slid, until Martha thought she couldn't walk no more. They come round a bend and Tommy seen a shadow in the road. Looked like an animal on its hind legs, or a child perhaps, with a peculiar shaped body and a square head.

"Martha whispered, 'What is it?'

"'Wait here. I'll check it out,' Tommy said.

"Sliding his feet in the slush, he inched forward. All of a sudden he begun to laugh. 'It's a mail box, for heaven's sake.'

"Martha smiled but she didn't find it funny. Tommy took her hand. 'Not too far now,' he said. 'There'll be a driveway and a house.' He lit a match to see the name on the box. He could only read the letters SCH.

"They moved up the drive towards the house, sure it would soon come into view. Feeling ahead with their feet, they was careful not to tumble into a hidden ditch. An awful smell carried on the wind; the stench what comes from old burned, decaying wood, rotting in dampness and mildew. They saw the outline of the house.

"'There's been a fire,' Tom said. 'I think there ain't nobody here.'

"'Let's go back, Tom; get out of here. I'm scared.'

"'Quiet.' Tom listened but he couldn't hear nothing above the howling storm. 'Let's take a look.'

"'No, Tom.'

"He ignored Martha. In the dim light, he crept towards the door, testing each step for broken boards. The wind grew quiet in the lee of the house. He peered through a broken panel in the door but couldn't see no light. He knocked; no answer. He tried again; still no answer. He raised his hand to feel the door. Suddenly; it crashed to the floor. A piece of glass shattered somewhere followed by a loud piercing scream. A noise so terrifying, they froze in fear. It echoed through the old house and died away in the distance. They crouched with tense nerves, panic-stricken, their bodies' like wild animals, alert for the least sign of movement. They was so tense, it seemed like the scream caused the storm to stop.

"In the dark corner by the chimney something moved. It come from above as if penetrating through the roof with a low whistling noise what increased like a whistle-kettle coming to the boil. Another terrible squawk sounded like a mix between an owl hooting and mule braying. Then an agonized human voice followed with a scream of torture.

"'Yooooo brooooooke my dooooor. Paaaay.'

"Martha shrieked. A hideous creature come towards them, its scream reaching a crescendo. The pointed white face scarred by fire was hairless except for flat whiskers tinged a dirty brown dangling from the chin. But the eyes! The eyes were the worst of all set on each side of a long protruding nose that looked like a beak. They were fiery red set in deep sockets on each side of the head. Reddish light shone from those eyes. Over the skull, it wore a woolen toque. The creature had no body, only a ghastly, billowing shadow, as wide as it was high, constantly shifting like a great dirty, gray, hovering bird. A nauseating stench filled the air.

"'Run,' Tommy shouted. 'Go quick! Hurry!'

"Martha leaped down the steps following their footprints through the slush. The creature chased her as far as the door, trapping Tommy inside. He shuffled backwards, the beast stalking him with its terrible squawk.

"'Paaaaay!' Then a throaty growl followed once more by 'Paaaaay! Paaaaay!'

"Tommy trembled, fearful the beast would attack. 'What do you want?'

"Once more, the beast screamed. Tommy inched back, never taking his eyes from the horror, feeling his way with his feet to avoid a tumble. He fumbled with his back pocket and found his wallet. He felt paper money, withdrew the first bill he touched and threw it in the air. The beast floated upward and shifted sideways chasing the money. Tommy saw a clear path to the door. He bolted forward. At the door, he stopped and looked back, wishing he had his camera.

"'Hurry up,' Martha bellowed but Tommy could not turn away.

"'Heeheehee,' screeched the figure.

LOST RIVER BRIDGE

"Out of the cloud came withered, gnarled claws grasping for the money. The bill almost reached the floor while those piercing red eyes searched for it. The gloating creature twisted and turned until it clutched the money. In the terrible red glow of the eyes, Tommy saw he had thrown a crisp, new, twenty-dollar bill. The cackling faded in the distance as he ran to catch his fleeing wife.

"They hurried down the road following the ruts until at last the lights shone in the distance. Eloise gave then a room in the Bed and Breakfast.

"Tell them what happened after that, Andy."

"The next morning," he began, "Tommy and Martha came to breakfast at the Fireside Café.

"'Well,' Eloise said, 'how did you get on?'

"'We smashed the truck,' Tommy said. 'Can I get a tow truck around here?'

"Curious glances swept through the restaurant. I was in my usual spot. I swiveled around on my stool and said, 'Is that right? Why don't you have a seat—get 'em some coffee, Eloise—and tell us like how many Mallow birds you seen up there in the hills.'

"'None,' Tommy said. 'But, we saw one horrendous ghost.'

"'A ghost? You don't say. Tell us about it.'

"Tommy told us what happened. There was a lot of open mouths and arched eyebrows, but nobody interrupted. Finally, he finished the story.

"'Them letters you saw on the mailbox,' somebody said, 'that's the Schumacher place. I think you folks is making this up.'

"'Just a minute, now,' I said. 'Y'all forgot it was Halloween last night. Kids was up there playing tricks, that's all. Come on folks, I'll drive you there so you can see there ain't nothing to it.'

"In the bright daylight, we could see their tracks from the night before. I showed them how the front wall was still standing, but, like Tommy said, the front door had fallen in. I could tell it happened the night before because it pushed the slush back aways. I led the way through the ruins and showed them the stone chimney with a piece of roof dangling from it. That was when I noticed there weren't no kids footprints in the slush. When I seen that, I knew for sure these folks was just making up this tale. It struck me as kind of strange. They didn't seem like the sort of folks who'd do something like that. 'Come on,' I said, 'let's get out of here.'

"When I turned to go, Martha was standing there with her face as white as the snow. She pointed her finger at the dangling roof by the chimney. 'Look,' she said.

"I walked across the room, and reached up on the brick corbel where she pointed. There was something there, all right.

"'Well, I'll be blessed,' I said, 'it's a coin purse. It's got Herman Schumacher name's sewn into it. What do you know 'bout that? No way that purse could have been setting there all these years, not with so many folks from the village coming here, especially them kids.'

"Martha had not moved. Her mouth hung open. She gaped at the purse. 'Open it, Andy,' she whispered.

"'Why? It's only an old-fashioned money purse,' I said

"'Open it, Andy. Have a look,' Tommy said.

"I snapped it open and pushed my finger inside. I stopped. 'Ain't that something,' I said. I pulled out a crisp, brand-new twenty-dollar bill."

Bill Hawkins turned to me.

"Ain't that a great story, Elijah? And you know it's a fact. Yes, sir, me and Andy was both there and seen it with our own eyes. It's an absolute fact; that's the last time it snowed in Ozark County in October."

On Friday morning, the postal carrier passed me on my way to Emery's house. For the first time in four days, he didn't have chains on his Jeep. I found Emery thumbing through the mail while Irene flipped the pages of the Ozark County Times.

"What are you doing today, Emery?"

"Pete and I are going to clean up around the church and get ready for Sunday. He's bringing the tractor."

Irene looked up from her paper. "Would you like to ask Pete home for lunch?"

"Thanks, Irene. That'd be nice."

Episode Nineteen

What About the Cemetery?

I rose from the kitchen table, hugged Irene, shook hands with Emery and expressed my thanks for a hearty breakfast. Emery appeared subdued, but walked with me to the church where I'd left my car during the storm. I felt tense for no reason I could identify. I sensed he was, too. It may have been simply because we didn't talk, which I found unusual for we always chattered about something. I opened the car door and turned to say goodbye. I cannot describe his expression. If I say sullen, it implies ill humor. I knew of nothing during my visit that displeased him. The loss of early blooms to old man winter could depress him, but he never mentioned it. Gloomy perhaps, or maybe tired? How could that be? We did hardly a stroke of work in the last few days. I was at a loss as I took his hand and looked into his eyes.

"Goodbye, Emery."

My tongue refused to utter more. Never had I experienced such a profound vulnerability to powers I could not control. In the few seconds we stared at each other, a deep affection welled up inside me. He did not smile, yet the upturn of the Taber mouth dispelled my suspicions.

"Goodbye, Elijah."

Without another word, he left me. I watched him enter the church. The door closed silently behind him.

Walter had asked me to visit before I returned home. I found him sitting alone in the café.

"Let's go," he said, "I've been waiting for you."

He bounced down the stairs like a teenager. We rounded the building and for the first time I saw the traffic barriers at the bridge. He led me beside the abutment to the edge of the water.

"Look there," he said.

A horizontal split extended from end to end of the bottom chord of the truss. It sagged about a foot at the center. Any vehicle crossing could easily cause a collapse.

"When did this happen?"

"I noticed the crack last fall. The snow did it in."

"I suppose the county owns it."

"Yep. And they'd love to give it away."

"So, what are you asking me?"

"Your opinion."

I didn't respond as we walked back to the Fireside Cafe. The sensible answer was obvious, yet I didn't want to say it. How did I become sentimental about this beautiful structure? Horse-drawn carriages, Abner's 1913 Model T, rusty pickup trucks, and at least one gas-guzzling Studebaker crossed my mind. I slouched into a chair as Eloise poured coffee. Walter sat across the table. I sighed and shook my head.

"It's over, Walter. Tell them you don't want it and let them tear it down."

"Well," Eloise said, "it's not over for me."

Walter's eyebrows raised and his eyes opened wide. "Meaning what?" He looked at his wife as if surprised she spoke at all. I might have suspected chauvinism except for the many times I heard them express affection for each other.

She positioned a chair backward at the end of the table, twisted her red baseball cap back to front and straddled the chair, miming the actions of a man distinct from those one would expect from a woman. Her arms folded over the backrest and her head moved from side to side, her eyes wide open as if about to reveal a secret after checking for anyone within earshot.

"Listen, guys, I knew this gal one time, see. Oh, she was a pipperoo, all right. Come from out-of-state, ain't exactly sure where from. She meets this fella, see, and they go walking in the

LOST RIVER BRIDGE

moonlight. It's a nice warm night and they're holding hands and all that lovey-dovey stuff. They come to a river, see. There's a bridge and they lean over the edge of the abutment and throw sticks in the water. He tells her a dumb story about the water flowing up hill. She thinks, what kind of nut does this guy think I am? He says, 'Watch,' and throws a stick in. When she sees it floating the wrong way, she gets so excited she throws her arms round his neck and kisses him. Well, ain't but one of us will ever know what was on this fella's mind, see, but he says to her, 'Will you marry me?' And she says, 'Yes.' And he says, 'The bridge will be a monument to our love and there better not ever be anybody tries to tear it down.' She thinks that's pretty. Romantic like, you know what I mean. So she says, 'Okay, here's the deal. No bridge, no love.' Now the question on the table, see, is whether this guy was just talking through his hat on account of what he had on his mind or if he truly meant it. What do you guys think?"

Walter said, "Shall we take a vote or do we want to change the subject?"

"No voting. The bridge is still there, see, so there ain't no problem yet. I got a hunch his gal is going to wait around and see what happens." She swung her legs off the chair and left.

Walter shrugged. "I want to show you something else."

Without explanation, he unrolled a huge drawing and twisted it around for me to read.

"I own most of this land. There's a few families haven't sold yet, but I hold the options. You can see the development is all on the south side. We won't need the old bridge anymore."

"And the Bed and Breakfast?"

"Going to tear it down."

I wondered if I had some kind of premonition when I said goodbye to Emery that morning. The meeting hall went long ago, a bulldozer could push away the remains of the Emporium in an hour, and there wasn't a house on the north side worth the cost of burning except Emery's. No, nothing worth saving except the toil of a solitary worker who devoted a lifetime tending to the Lord God as best he could.

"Walter, I wonder if you'd go halfers with me on the cost of a special gift. I'd like to put a steeple on the church. They fabricate them in sheet metal these days. A couple of thousand dollars, I imagine. If you'll pay half, then I'm going to install a bell."

He squinted at me, his head nodding slightly, not in agreement but deep in concentration. He looked away, then glanced at Eloise. She filled his coffee cup.

"It'd be a nice gesture," she said.

"Yeah, I suppose so," Walter said. "Problem is, if the bridge goes, won't be anybody uses the church. Too bad it's on the wrong side."

I turned away, discouraged with the realization he was right. "You could move the church," I said.

"Sure we could, and the memorial for the Vietnam soldiers, but that's not the problem. What do we do about the cemetery?"

I didn't enjoy my evening because I had not answered Walter's question. I couldn't; I didn't have an answer. Frieda had been in her grave since 1830; Granny Sarah since 1841. My thoughts dwelled on Elijah Pursey, Abby Watson and hundreds of others sharing eternity in the Sarah Taber Memorial Cemetery. The decision was not mine to make and brooding would not change anything. The future lay in the hands of Walter Applehorn. I wondered what he'd do. It was a sad time for me, but the worst was yet to come.

I awoke to the ring of the telephone. That was unusual. I received few calls; none at six o'clock in the morning.

"Hello."

"Elijah?"

"Yes."

"This is Irene."

"Irene! What are—"

"Emery died last night. Quietly. In his sleep. His heart gave out. He woke me and took my hand. Without a word, he closed his eyes and breathed his last."

Episode Twenty

The Disciples

Irene and I sat in the front pew gazing toward the open casket. She told me earlier the ordeal of the visitation did not perturb her. She'd known everybody in the community since she was a little girl. Walter, Eloise and perhaps one or two other more recent residents were sure to be on hand, but even those folks she had known for at least fifteen years. Emery had no friends outside the community, save a few pastors from the County Ministerial Alliance. Of course, young Jeremy Hawkins would conduct the service. He was a local boy who attended seminary, and returned to serve in the Presbyterian Church in West Plains. He regarded Emery as his mentor. They spend many hours together.

She twisted sideways, and took my right hand in both of hers. "Do you remember the day you came back?"

Her question woke me from my daydream. "Strange that you should ask. I was thinking about that day. I waited in the vestibule regretting I had not warned you of my arrival."

"When was that?"

"Early October last year."

"Yes." She continued to hold my hand as I waited for her to reveal her thoughts. In a moment, her head turned towards the casket, and her hands fell away from mine. Her voice was soft and tender. She was no longer talking to me.

"On Thursday, before Elijah came, we were sitting in the kitchen. Do you remember? You were reading the Ozark County Times. You spoke from behind the paper so matter-of-factly I thought you were reading to me. 'Elijah will be here on Sunday,' you said. I said, 'Is it in the paper?' You didn't answer and I was sorry. I said so and still you didn't answer."

She turned back to me. "I knew when you stepped out from the vestibule that day, you regretted not having warned me you were coming. But you see, he warned me. Over the years, he told me many things that would happen and he was often right. When I was little, I marveled at his sense of the future. I accepted it as I grew older, not challenging his premonitions, and never ever saying a word if he was wrong. I asked him once to teach me how to do it. He said it couldn't be taught. He said it was something inside him. He could feel it, especially when he was in the cemetery. That's why he wanted the caretaker's job when he was fifteen.

"When I said I was sorry for asking about your visit, he understood my apology as a challenge. Throughout his life, people everywhere disbelieved him. They talked about coincidence, good guesses and lucky hunches. He felt lonely all his life. After his mother died, it became worse. I had to fill the void she left, and the only way I could succeed was never to challenge his predictions, his conversations with the ants, his visions of the dead. When you came the first time in 1942, he thought you would be another laugher, chiding what people called his foolishness. And maybe you did, I don't know, but you had the good sense never to do it to his face. After we married, he told me he asked you many times if you believed him. You always reassured him, saying you did. You never challenged, even his wildest stories. I'm not talking about tanker fish and dogs that talk. I'm talking about his visions and his dreams. Silly as it sounds, you won him over the night you told the story of Charlie Castor. He loved that story, and he loved you."

"Good Lord, Irene!" The exclamation escaped me before I could stop it. "I had no idea he felt that way."

"It's true. He regarded you as more than a friend. He regarded you as a disciple."

"I don't know what to say."

"Don't say anything. You don't need to because I understand. You see, he thought of me as a disciple, too. And that's the way he felt about Jeremy Hawkins."

LOST RIVER BRIDGE

I left Irene after supper and returned to the Bed and Breakfast where I found a wake in progress; a storytelling wake, no less. One by one, the men told of experiences with Emery or related a favorite story from his repertoire. I enjoyed the tales, delivered with genuine compassion and respect, not ridicule. Walter Applehorn took the floor.

"I see Elijah Taber is here now," he began. My first fear was he'd ask me to speak. I didn't want to and decided I would simply decline his offer. It wasn't storytelling time for me, but I knew it was their way of honoring a friend.

"I wasn't here in 1946," Walter continued, "but it is my understanding that Elijah told a story about a great Canadian named Charlie Castor. He chummed around with a moose. Elijah, what was the name of that moose?"

"Orignal," I shouted.

"Orignal! I remember now. Well, after Elijah returned to Canada, Emery wanted to make sure Elijah wasn't fibbing a story about this Castor fellow. He wanted to make sure it was true. He did some research and uncovered some interesting facts.

"You all know Charlie was a beaver trapper. Beaver hats and collars were popular in England at that time; a perfect market for Charlie, but it took near a year to get the pelts to market from the Canadian hinterland. All the while he dug out Hudson's Bay, Charlie worried about a better way.

"After the glacier melted, he figured it out. He sent his helper to get the biggest sea-going vessel available. He told him to load it with wood chips, sawdust, and anything else the beavers would eat. 'Then set sail for the old country, but don't dock in England,' he said. 'You sail north to Scotland and somewhere up around the Orkney Islands, you dump the beaver food in the ocean.'

"His helper thought Charlie was crazy, but it wasn't his money so he shrugged his shoulders and said, 'Okay.' But Charlie wasn't crazy. He knew the gulf steam swept across the Atlantic Ocean, up the east coast of Scotland and back to the west again across the top of the world.

"While his helper sailed across the ocean, Charlie filled Hudson's Bay with beavers and kept them hungry. When the food came floating over, Charlie turned the beavers loose. Why, those animals were so hungry, they ate their way clean across the ocean in less than a week. They loved it because they'd never had their feed salted before.

"Now some of you may think there's no truth in this tale, but I'm here to tell you, you're wrong. Emery told me he'd seen the proof with his own eyes. After Charlie's helper dumped the feed in the ocean, he had to find more wood to keep the beavers coming. The only recourse was to chop down the trees. Emery said in the Orkney Islands, there isn't a tree in sight. The other proof lay on the roofs on the houses. Every home had nice looking brown shingles with round edges. Those roofing shingles were beaver tails the helper sold."

Walter took my arm and dragged me to my feet. "Did you know Emery had half a dozen stories about Charlie Castor, all of them true because he saw the proof with his own eyes?" He shook my hand. "Your turn," he whispered.

I stood in silence for a few moments gathering my thoughts. I looked around the room and saw sadness in many an eye.

"I've been honored today in a way I never imagined. Earlier, Irene Taber informed me, much to my surprise, how much Emery enjoyed my story of Charlie Castor told forty-three years ago on the night he announced their wedding plans. Tonight, I learned that Emery made Charlie Castor a real person, as real as Paul Bunyon who, as everybody in this room knows, lived and breathed in a time gone by that will never return. Thank you, Emery."

In the morning, Irene, Jeremy, and I met at the church. We sat in silence as the sound of the gravedigger clawing at the stones floated through the open windows. Jeremy offered a prayer. Afterwards, we picked flowers from Emery's spring garden and arranged the church for the two o'clock service.

I happened to be in the northeast corner of the cemetery clipping some greenery for the flower arrangement when a sudden movement flashed in the corner of my eye. I looked around. An elderly couple closed their car door, and I assumed I'd seen a reflection of sunlight. I turned back to continue my work when I saw a man standing twenty feet away at the edge of the woods. He was round-shouldered with a ragged suit coat, patched at the elbows, pulled around his slight frame, his arms crossed above the waist as if he were cold. Long strands of gray hair covered his ears. A wide mustache drooped from the corners of his mouth, the ends disappearing in a scraggy gray beard. He wore calf-height rubber boots with blue jeans tucked inside. The knee patches were colorful bits of cloth sewn at odd angles. His face was that of a wild animal, eyes darting everywhere, his body tense and alert, ready to bolt at the slightest threat. I recognized Jack Polecat.

My mind raced to thoughts of Granny Sarah and Frieda and the Schumacher fire and Abby Watson and I wanted to leap the fence and capture him, lasso him, and drag him to Irene before he could escape. I quelled my excitement, and spoke as casually as I could master.

"Hello."

He nodded.

"Would you like to come to the church?"

I took a step. He shrank back into the shadows of the trees.

"It's all right. I won't hurt you."

His eyes shifted both ways before he stepped forward.

"Walk done by the house. There's no one there."

He took two cautious steps.

"May I walk with you? I'll stay on this side of the fence."

He nodded.

He walked towards the road, turned half-sideways with his leading shoulder against the wall. At the flowerbed, he moved from the house and finally reached the road. I angled away from the fence, holding the shears behind me where he couldn't see them. I wiggled them back and forth, hoping to reflect a ray of light that would capture Irene's attention. I glanced over my shoulder. She stood on the side entrance walk with the new arrivals.

"Irene is over there. I think she's talking with some friends. Do you see her?"

He nodded.

"Do you want to talk to her?"

He shook his head. His back straightened slightly, and he seemed more resolute as if, have gotten this far, he was determined to carry out his mission, whatever it was. His eyes were no less shifty as we approached the church, he on the road, me fifteen feet away on the grass.

Irene had not seen my signal. Her head turned. She caught sight of the two of us. Both her hands jerked to her face, and I heard a stifled scream. She wavered. The man grabbed her as she crumpled. He staggered under her dead weight. I flew across the few feet separating us and caught them before they tumbled to the ground.

"Irene! It's all right. Irene!" I turned to the visitors. "Madam. Would you be kind enough to get a glass of water from the church?" Before she could move, Jeremy appeared with water in a plastic bottle. I put it to Irene's lips.

"Good Lord!" I could scarcely hear Irene's whisper above her gasping for air. "Where is he?"

I turned. The road was empty.

"Jeremy, take our visitors behind the church, please! You'll excuse me, I hope. I don't mean to be rude but this is a most traumatic moment for Irene." I hoped they understood, but there was no time to explain. "Come with me, Irene. Quietly. Don't say a word."

I kept my arm around her, leading the way to the road, past the wrought iron fencing, and up the cobblestone walk. We mounted the steps silently, stepped through the vestibule, and stopped.

The visitor stood immobile beside the open casket. He stared at the corpse. I wasn't sure, but I thought I saw a head movement, the kind one makes when talking. I felt Irene tug against my grasp. I held her firmly and signaled to be quiet.

"In a moment," I whispered. "Watch."

Presently, the head moved to right and left. Then again. And a third time. At last, the right hand reached out to touch the corpse. The left hand reached into the jacket pocket. A fumbling action followed as both hands reached into the coffin. Irene could stand no more. She tore herself from my grip and ran up the aisle.

"Lou! Lou! Lou!" She kept repeating his name over and over.

At the sound of her voice, Lou Pursey wheeled about. Before he could move, she encircled him in her arms, and clung to him leaving no escape. His eyes fell on mine, and I felt a terrible pain. The fear I saw so many years ago was still there. I walked forward.

"Come," I said. "Let's go outside to the garden."

I spent the early afternoon as a guardian, a job I did not want, but could not refuse. Irene clung to Lou refusing to let him free for one moment. I knew she felt he would run away if she left him. As the time approached for the service, she assigned me the task of looking after Lou. She and Jeremy stood in the vestibule greeting the mourners. I sat in the front pew with Lou. We did not talk. I felt he had resigned himself, perhaps with some relief, to the inescapable situation he was in.

Jeremy, clad in his white surplice, came down the side aisle. Walking past the casket, he came to an abrupt halt. He stared at the corpse, then turned to me. "Come here," he said.

"I can't." I nodded towards Lou.

Jeremy slid into the pew. "Go have a look," he said.

I rose and peered into the coffin. Incredible. I whispered to Jeremy. "Stay here. I have to tell Irene. I'll be right back."

In the vestibule, I interrupted Irene in mid sentence. "Excuse me, I apologize." I'm afraid my smile was rather weak. "I must speak to you privately, for a moment."

"All right," she said. "What is it?"

Her reaction surprised me. Not because of the decision she made, but because she made it instantaneously as if the development were without surprise. "Leave it there," she said.

I returned to my seat. Before Jeremy left, he leaned across in front of Lou to ask, "What is it?"

"It's Granny Sarah's St. Christopher medallion."

Jeremy conducted a simple service in an elegant and reverential manner. It started with a rendition of "Onward Christian Soldiers" that brought back memories of Emery striding down the aisle, cross in one hand, Bible in the other. Then the undertaker closed the casket. The pallbearers carried it out the front door with Irene following, clutching Lou on her right side and me on her left. With the congregation gathered round, the graveside ceremony was beautiful. It followed the Presbyterian ritual shortened somewhat because it was outside. There were no eulogies. "Those took place last night in the Fireside Café," Jeremy explained to the mourners who may not have attended the storytelling. Then he sang the Lord's Prayer in his robust voice not unlike Emery's. In an emotional ceremony, Emery was buried beside his idol, Elijah Taber Pursey.

    We gathered at Emery's home after the service. In the tradition of the mountains, the neighbors had brought enough food to feed an army. As Lou's guardian, I was not aware who had attended until the reception. One of the first strangers I met was Timothy. He was everything Irene said he was and more; loquacious, humorous and lovable. Unknown to me, an affinity existed between Lou and him, although I suspected an attachment existed between Timothy and anybody he ever met. He latched on to Lou, and worked his miracle by escorting him around the room telling childhood tales, assigning escapades to Lou that probably never happened.
    Annie and Rachel were there. Later, Irene told me that Annie gave her the letter. "It's wonderful," she said. "It's a long letter all about Ezra, Levi and their families. I'll be able to complete a lot of the missing genealogy in Elijah Pursey's family Bible, maybe even locate some of his descendants."

    In the evening, Irene, Lou, Jeremy and I walked through the cemetery. "Let's go to the corner, the far corner where Granny Sarah holds her picnics."
    We stood under the tree while I did my best imitation of Emery staring off into space with unblinking eyes. "Goodbye Granny Sarah, Frieda. Goodbye, Emery."
    In a moment, I came out of my trance. "Frieda is wearing the medallion round her neck. Emery is taking them home."

STEPHEN P. BYERS

Stephen P. Byers was born in Montreal, Quebec in 1924, the youngest of five children. He served in the Canadian Army from 1943 to 1946. After the war he earned a Civil Engineer degree from McGill University. In 1972, he moved to Kansas City to work on the construction of a major commercial project.

In 1989, he retired to Bella Vista, Arkansas where he joined the Tellers of Tales, a storytelling group associated with the Shiloh Museum of Ozark History where he was inspired to write his own stories.

Stephen is married to Mary Elspeth Rankine. They have four children and six grandchildren.

Stephen's two prior books are *The Naked Jaybird* and *Bent Coin*. More information about him and his books may be found at http://www.booksbybyers.com.

WHAT READERS HAVE SAID

Lost River Bridge is a charming series of Ozark tales … Stephen Byers is a storyteller extraordinaire. This book is a gem.
Signe A. Dayhoff, Ph.D., psychologist and author

… a fascinating look at Ozark folk life through stories told by people of Lost River Bridge … Stephen Byers has cemented his reputation as a master storyteller.
Bob Besom, Director, Shiloh Museum of Ozark History

Stephen Byers is a wonderful storyteller …
Barbara Fritchman Thompson, librarian & research specialist.

Stephen Byers tells compelling tales about a community you will want to visit …
Kyle Hannon, author

Good old country yarns told with gentle good humor.
Shel Horowitz, author

Turn right at the dog! … yarns spun with such graphic detail you feel you are there ... Lost River Bridge shows the true essence of the Ozarks. I know; I lived within a stones throw of the setting of this book.
Kathy Rapp, reviewer

Stephen Byers does a fantastic job of connecting the diverse characters with a common thread of human emotion. The characters are so real, their plights believable. In a world of diversity, it is refreshing to have a work that reminds the reader of the commonalities between people of all walks of life.
Lisa Rene Reynolds, psychotherapist, author

The full text of each endorsement may be read at
http://www.booksbybyers.com/lost_river_bridge.html#reviews